TWO WEEKS WITH THE QUEEN

Born in the UK, Morris Gleitzman moved to Australia with his family at the age of sixteen. His career took off as a screenwriter and a newspaper columnist before he became a successful author. He has written a number of children's books including *Misery Guts*, *Worry Warts*, *Blabber Mouth* and *Puppy Fat*. He now lives in Sydney and has two children.

Books by Morris Gleitzman

Two Weeks with the Queen
Misery Guts
Worry Warts
Puppy Fat
Blabber Mouth
Sticky Beak
Belly Flop
Water Wings

With Mary Morris

Two Weeks with the Queen – The Play

Morris Gleitzman

Two Weeks With The Queen

MACMILLAN
CHILDREN'S BOOKS

For Christine

First published 1989 by Blackie & Son Limited

This edition published 1995 by Macmillan Children's Books,
a division of Macmillan Publishers Limited
25 Eccleston Place London SW1W 9NF
and Basingstoke

Associated companies throughout the world

ISBN 0 330 31376 2

17 19 18 16

A CIP catalogue record for this book is available
from the British Library

Printed and bound in Great Britain

Chapter One

The Queen looked out across the Mudfords' living room and wished everyone a happy Christmas.

Colin scowled.

Easy for you, he thought. Bet you got what you wanted. Bet if you wanted a microscope you got a microscope. Bet your tree was covered with microscopes. Bet nobody gave you daggy school shoes for Christmas.

Colin looked away from the Queen's flickering face on the TV screen and down at the shiny black shoes peeping up at him from their box on the threadbare carpet.

Yuk.

The Queen obviously couldn't see them because she continued her Christmas Message without once chucking up.

'. . . ridding our world of suffering and pain is not an easy goal,' she was saying, 'but we will achieve that goal if it is our sincere wish.'

Colin's sincere wish was that the shoes would burst into flames and explode into pieces. But they didn't, even though they were being shot at by a low-flying MiG fighter plane.

Colin stared out the window at the dusty paddocks. The shimmering glare was painful to look at, but not as painful as the sight of Luke playing happily with his model plane. Why should that little whinger get exactly what he wanted, right down to the colour of the pilot's helmet and the number of napalm canisters under the wings?

It wasn't fair.

'. . . fair share of the world's resources for all her people,' the Queen was saying.

Colin looked at his parents. He hoped the Queen was making them feel guilty.

It didn't look as though she was. People who are riddled with guilt don't usually cuddle up on the settee and fan each other with bits torn off a beer carton.

Colin stared at them for a while but that didn't plunge them into guilt either, so he went back to watching the Queen.

He wondered what it would be like to be that important. So important that it didn't even matter if you spoke like a total prawn, millions of people all over the world would still sit down on Christmas afternoon and say shhhh and listen to you.

In his head, Colin started composing a letter. 'Dear Your Majesty The Queen, I would be very grateful if you could send some tips on how to grab people's attention and make them listen to you, understand what you want for Christmas etc. Even though I'm twelve I might as well be a lump of wood for all the attention I get around this place. Also some tips on how to stop younger brothers getting everything. I understand that chopping their heads off has been used a bit in your family. This is frowned on in Australia so something legal please . . . '

Several loud explosions echoed around the shoe box as Luke roared in for another attack on the aircraft carrier HMS Yukky School Shoes.

'Luke,' said Mum, 'we're trying to listen to the Queen.'

'I don't feel well,' said Luke.

Serves you right, thought Colin, for having three lots of ice-cream with your Chrissie pud.

'Serves you right,' said Mum, 'for having four lots of ice-cream with your Chrissie pud.'

Four? Colin couldn't believe his ears. When he was eight he'd only been allowed two. Young kids today didn't know how well off they were.

'I feel sick,' said Luke.

'Try keeping the racket down a bit,' said Dad, 'and you'll feel better.'

'Probably a strain of heat-resistant bacteria in the Chrissie pud,' said Colin. 'Pity we haven't got a microscope in the family, I could have run some tests and spotted it.'

Colin saw Mum and Dad swap a little glance that he wasn't meant to see.

They knew. They actually knew what he was busting for and they'd still given him shoes. Boy, wait till he had time to write that anonymous letter to the child welfare department.

Luke came over and held out the MiG in a skinny hand.

'Wanna go?'

Colin shook his head. That's all he needed, charity from an eight year old.

Luke's pale brow furrowed for a second, then he was away, inflicting serious artillery damage to an already battered cane chair.

A gust of scorching wind swept in from the Western Plains and made the plastic branches of the Christmas tree flap wildly. Something in the kitchen started to bang.

'Col, shut that screen door, old mate,' said Dad.

Colin dragged himself to his feet.

'Luke'd get there quicker,' he muttered, 'he's got turbo thrusters and I've only got lace-ups.'

But Mum and Dad's eyes were already glued back on the TV screen.

'. . . in these difficult times,' the Queen was saying, 'we have to work and struggle for privilege and good fortune.'

'Bull,' said Colin loudly as he slouched out to the kitchen, 'some people are born with it.'

Mum and Dad stared at the Queen.

Colin stared at Luke.

As Colin wedged a chicken bone under the screen door to stop it flapping open again, he heard the music playing at the end of the Queen's Christmas

Message. Then he heard footsteps behind him. He straightened up. It was Mum and Dad.

Mum gave a little cough to clear her throat.

'Love,' she said, 'about the microscope . . .'

'Next time, eh?' said Dad.

They looked at Colin.

Colin looked at them.

He could hear Luke in the lounge, shooting enemy planes out of the sky with a faint roar.

'We just couldn't stretch to one this time,' said Mum, 'not with you needing a new pair of good shoes and all. But don't forget, it's your birthday in less than five months.'

And it's Luke's birthday in less than two months, thought Colin bitterly. Wonder what he'll get? A working model of the Jervis Bay Naval Depot with matching aircraft carriers? A trip round the world? A car?

'They're pretty snazzy shoes,' Dad was saying. 'Bloke could end up Prime Minister in shoes like those.'

'I've got shoes.' Colin pointed down to his brown elastic-sided boots. OK, they were a bit scuffed from when he'd borrowed Doug Beale's trail-bike and the brakes had failed and he'd had to use his feet to stop, but they'd rub up with a bit of spit and chicken fat.

Dad sighed.

'Wish we could all wear boots,' he said, 'but if you want people to take notice of you in this world, you've got to dress proper and wear decent shoes. Look at me with the Wheat Board. Luke was born on the Sunday, I got the shoes on the Monday, landed the job on the Tuesday arvo.'

Dad grinned and gave Colin a pretend punch in the guts. Colin tried to smile but his face felt like uncooked Chrissie pud.

Mum looked at him closely, concerned.

'Love, is there anything else?'

Colin was still trying to work out how to explain without sounding like the one thing Dad hated (a whinger) when they heard the thump from the lounge.

They hurried in.

Luke lay on the floor, eyes closed, very pale, very still.

Chapter Two

The ambulance men grunted as they lifted the stretcher into the ambulance.

'Weighs a bit for a young'un,' one of them muttered.

Mum and Dad, watching anxiously, didn't say anything so Colin decided he'd better explain.

'It's all the food in his digestive tract. Nine turkey nuggets and four lots of Christmas pudding. His large intestine's probably blocking the flow of blood to his brain.'

The ambulance men, who'd been half-way through a fourth helping of Christmas pudding themselves at the station and were keen to get back to it, ignored him.

'You can faint from overeating,' said Colin. 'It's a medical fact. I've done it with jelly snakes.'

One of the ambulance men helped Colin's mother into the ambulance while the other helped a nurse tuck a blanket round Luke's legs.

'Don't worry yourself, Mrs Mudford,' said the nurse. She checked Luke's pulse. 'He'll be right. Probably just the excitement of the season.'

'We've warned him about going on bombing raids straight after meals,' said Colin, climbing into the ambulance.

The nurse blocked his way.

'Sorry, young man, full up.'

Colin glared at her. What a nerve. Specially as she worked part-time in the cake shop on Saturday mornings and probably sold Mum the Chrissie pud in the first place.

'You go with your Dad,' said one of the ambulance men, lifting Colin down like a sack of old bandages. He shut the rear doors and trotted round to the cab.

'Come on, fair go,' Colin called after him. 'I've never been in an ambulance. Where's your Christmas spirit?'

It was obviously back at the station with the Christmas pudding because the ambulance sped away down the street leaving Colin with a mouthful of dust.

Behind him, Dad blew the horn and signalled tensely for him to get into the car.

Colin sighed.

Next Christmas he was going to stuff himself stupid.

Colin peered down the rubber tube. At the other end the whole world was a tiny circle. In the centre of that circle was Luke, surrounded by most of the nurses and doctors in western New South Wales.

Well, one doctor and three nurses. And a couple of pieces of important-looking medical equipment that

Luke, twisting round in bed, was gazing at with fascination.

Colin watched as the nurses and the important-looking medical equipment all hummed and winked and made a fuss of Luke.

Then everything went black.

At last, thought Colin, my turn.

He waited for more symptoms to appear and for the nurses to rush over and start making a fuss of him.

But it wasn't Peruvian measles or Upper Congo Swine Fever, it was only the doctor stepping in front of the rubber tube.

'Hey, come on, that's not a toy.'

The doctor grabbed the rubber tube and steered Colin out of the ward.

'Any idea what it is yet?' asked Colin. 'I reckon it's gastric. If it'll help you put your finger on it I can tell you what he's eaten today. One bowl of Coco-Pops, three jelly snakes, some licorice allsorts, packet of Minties, six gherkins, half a bowl of Twisties and a chocolate Santa. That was before lunch. Would you like me to write this all down?'

The doctor didn't answer. Colin wondered if many doctors went deaf from sticking their stethoscopes too far into their ears.

Mum and Dad were sitting in the waiting area anxiously chewing their bottom lips.

'How is he, doctor?' asked Mum.

The doctor seemed to hear that OK.

'The young lad's looking much brighter now, Mr

and Mrs Mudford,' he said. 'We've sent a blood sample down to pathology in Sydney so we'll know the full story in a couple of days. I don't think it's anything to worry about. Happy Christmas.'

With a jingle of car keys and a glance at his watch he was gone.

Dad squeezed Mum's hand.

'See, nothing to worry about,' he said.

'I know,' she replied.

'That's a relief,' he said.

'Yes,' she said.

Neither of them looked relieved to Colin. He watched them still chewing their bottom lips. It's not fair, he thought, making people wait for tests to come all the way back from Sydney. Specially just for gastric. I mean I know this is only a small country hospital, but Mum and Dad are parents and parents can't help worrying. It's a fact of nature, like monkeys eating their own poos.

Colin had a sudden vision of how grateful Mum and Dad would be if someone could check out Luke's blood now, this afternoon.

The matron called Mum and Dad into her office to take care of the paperwork.

Colin decided that while they were doing that he'd take care of other things.

'No,' said Luke, pulling the covers over his head.

'I don't need a bottleful or anything, just a tiny bit,' whispered Colin.

He looked around to make sure none of the nurses were watching.

'Come on, it won't hurt.'

'It will,' said Luke's muffled voice.

Colin took a deep breath. How could a kid who was always falling out of trees and dripping blood all over the house be so sooky about handing over a bit now?

He put his mouth to where he thought Luke's ear was.

'It's for Mum and Dad.'

Luke's voice sounded faint under the covers. 'I gave them placemats.'

There was a pause, then an arm slowly slid out from under the sheet.

Colin grabbed it, pushed up the pyjama sleeve and hunted for a not-too-old scab.

It was a top microscope, but Colin didn't have time to admire it. The little room it was sitting in was on the main corridor of the hospital and someone could walk in at any time.

He pulled out his hanky, found Luke's blood-spot, and slid it under the lens. He peered into the microscope and focused it.

Wriggly things, that's what he was looking for. Like when they'd looked at the frog under the microscope in science and there'd been a million little wriggly things which Mr Blair reckoned were germs on account of the frog having been dead for two weeks because Arnie Strachan had put it in his lunchbox and lost the lunchbox.

Colin couldn't see any wriggly things in Luke's blood.

Just blobs.

He figured gastric germs would probably be wriggly rather than blobby.

He peered at Luke's blood again. Not a wriggle.

What I need, he thought, is some healthy blood to compare it to.

Without hesitating (if he was sprung, that matron looked like she could remove an appendix with her teeth) Colin grabbed a pin and jabbed it into his finger. He put a spot of his own blood onto his hanky, slid it under the lens and peered at it.

Wriggle.

Wriggle wriggle.

His blood was full of wriggly things.

Colin felt the rest of his blood pounding in his head. He had a vision of Mum and Dad kneeling by his bed holding his hands and weeping while several hundred doctors and nurses wheeled huge and very important-looking pieces of medical equipment into position.

Then he had a very different vision. Of him telling Mum and Dad and them not believing him.

What I need, he decided, is a second opinion.

By the time he got to the doctor's house he was in a fair bit of pain.

It was his new shoes, rubbing the backs of his

ankles. He'd had to wear them because that was his excuse for going for a walk, to try them out.

Another bit of him was hurting as well, the bit inside that always ached when Mum and Dad did something that made him think they preferred Luke. It had started this time as soon as Mum had said, 'Good idea, love, you take yourself off for an hour, give me and Dad a chance to get some of Luke's things together and take them to the hospital.'

They'd be sorry when they found out it was him who was really sick.

He checked a brass number on a smart polished-wood mailbox and turned into the doctor's driveway.

The doctor lived on the side of town where people had brick houses with front lawns and sprinklers and two toilets. Dad reckoned this was a criminal waste of water. Colin reckoned that if people were clever and successful and important it was OK. As long as they didn't show off about it, like inviting two people in to go to the toilet at once.

He knocked on the doctor's big, stained-glass front door. The doctor opened it. He was wearing a party hat and a red plastic nose and holding a turkey leg.

From inside Colin could hear Christmas music and lots of adults and children talking and laughing.

He held out his hanky with the blood spots on it.

'Sorry to bother you,' he said, 'but I think I've got gastric.'

The doctor stared. Then he took off his red plastic nose.

* * *

Later, when the doctor drove Colin home in his silver Jag, Colin had got over not having gastric.

At first it had been a bitter blow, but interesting as well, the doctor getting out his microscope and showing Colin the wriggly things that covered not only the blood spot but that entire corner of the hanky.

The doctor had asked Colin if his hanky had come into contact with a dead animal and Colin had said, yes, sort of, Arnie Strachan had used it to wipe out his lunchbox.

Then the doctor had explained that the wriggly things had only got onto Colin's blood spot because they were on the hanky in the first place.

Colin had asked why the wriggly things hadn't got onto Luke's blood spot and the doctor had said because by some miracle Luke's corner of the hanky had stayed clean.

Well, cleanish.

As they turned into Colin's street, Colin glanced across at the doctor. They knew their stuff, these medical blokes. The doctor saw him looking. He gave Colin a grin.

'Bit of a pain, eh, having your kid brother in hospital. Bloke gets a bit ignored when his kid brother's in hospital.'

Colin didn't say anything. He wondered if the doctor would agree to swap brains with Dad. The first double brain transplant in Australia. Probably not.

'Don't worry about your brother,' said the doctor. 'He'll be out of hospital in a couple of days.'

Colin hoped the doctor was right.

He looked around the car as they purred along. The leather seats, the real wood dashboard, the aerial that went up without you having to stop the car and get out and pull at it and swear like with Dad's.

Of course he's right, thought Colin. You don't get a car like this by being wrong.

Chapter Three

Most mornings Colin woke up because Luke climbed onto the chest of drawers and jumped on him. On Boxing Day morning he woke up for different reasons.

(1) He felt strange and unusual. It took him a while to realise this was because Luke wasn't jumping on him.

(2) The band-aids on his heels had come loose and were tickling his feet.

(3) Mum was yelling on the phone right outside his door.

'He's OK,' she was shouting, 'they've taken a blood sample and we're waiting for the results.'

Colin could tell from the shouting that it was the Christmas phone call from Aunty Iris and Uncle Bob in England.

'No, no, completely out of the blue,' Mum yelled. 'One minute he was fine, the next he was on the floor.'

Colin lay in bed and listened. It wasn't skickybeaking because even if he put bubble-gum in his ears and stuck his head under the pillow he'd hear every word.

'No, didn't throw up but he was real white and everything,' shouted Mum.

Colin wondered if Mrs Baker next door could hear. Probably, and she was staying with her son in Perth.

'Ambulance,' yelled Mum. 'Yes, that's right.'

Must be a bad line. Though now he thought about it Mum always shouted during Aunty Iris and Uncle Bob's Christmas phone call. Perhaps Aunty Iris and Uncle Bob were a bit deaf. Or ringing from a disco.

'Didn't want to be left at first,' yelled Mum, 'but then we took him in his MiG.'

He'd never met them, but they seemed like nice people.

'MiG.'

They always rang at Christmas and asked how everyone was, including him.

'M, small i, big G,' shouted Mum. 'We gave it to him. That's right. OK. I'll let you know. Bye. Love to you all. Bye.'

Except this year Mum hadn't mentioned him once.

'Mmmm, I'm starving.'

Colin stared.

Dad poured out his Nutri-Grain and said it again.

'Starving.'

Why's he saying that, thought Colin. He's never said 'Mmmm I'm starving' before, not in all the breakfasts I've known him. 'I'm empty as a creek at Christmas', yes, and even 'I could eat a horse with the jockey still on it' if he's in a good mood, but never 'Mmmm I'm starving'.

'Me too,' said Mum.

Colin couldn't believe his ears.

Me too?

Me too?

Never in his entire life had he heard Mum say 'Me too'. It was always 'Me included'.

'I like Kentucky Fried better than McDonald's,' you'd say.

'Me included,' she'd say.

'But it's still given me a pain in the gut,' you'd add.

'Me included,' she'd say.

Rumour had it that at their wedding Dad had said, 'I do,' and Mum had said, 'Me included.'

So what was all this 'Me too'?

Then Colin realised what was going on. They were putting on a Brave Face. It was what adults did when they were frightened.

Kids could cry, or throw up, or stay in bed and not talk to anyone, or even panic and scream 'Help' at the top of their lungs like he and Luke had done the time Dad left them in the car at the back of the hardware shop and didn't say how long he'd be.

Adults had to put on a Brave Face.

You saw them all the time in cars, waiting for people who hadn't said how long they'd be. They'd never be crying or screaming, just sitting there with a Brave Face. If there were two of them they might be talking, lips moving behind the glass.

Colin now realised that what they were probably saying was, 'Mmmm, I'm starving' and 'Me too'.

He watched Mum and Dad eat their Nutri-Grain. They were pretty good at putting on Brave Faces, even managing tight little smiles to each other.

'Don't worry,' said Colin, 'the doctor said Luke'll be out of hospital in a couple of days.'

Dad put his hand on Colin's arm and gave it a squeeze. 'Thanks, old mate.'

Colin felt like he'd just won ten dollars in a lottery.

'You're a good kid,' said Mum. 'Sorry we yelled a bit yesterday when the doc brought you home. We were talking about it after and, well, that was a pretty top act, going round there cause you were worried about Lukie. Good on you.' She ruffled his hair.

It felt so good Colin decided not to complicate it by mentioning the wriggly things and Arnie Strachan's lunchbox.

Mum went back to her breakfast. A sigh escaped between mouthfuls. Dad gave her a squeeze.

'The doc knows what he's talking about, love. Couple of days and Luke'll be falling out of trees with the best of 'em.'

Mum stared at Dad in mock horror. 'Ray,' she said, and flicked a Nutri-Grain at him.

'All right,' said Dad, grinning, 'um . . . catching snakes with the best of 'em.'

Mum rolled her eyes and pretended to strangle Dad.

'Playing cricket,' said Colin.

'That's it,' said Mum. 'Good on you, Col.'

* * *

Colin glanced around to see that all his fieldsmen were in position, then ran up and bowled a medium-paced offspinner.

It was a bit short and Luke stepped forward, swung the bat and clouted the ball over Colin's head.

'Catch,' shouted Colin to the fieldsman on the boundary.

The fieldsman lunged upwards, but it was too high and he would have fallen out of bed if his leg hadn't been encased in plaster and wired to a pulley.

'Six,' shouted Luke as the ball bounced off the end wall of the ward and landed in a bowl of grapes.

Everyone in the ward clapped and Colin had to admit it was a pretty good hit, even though he wasn't bowling his best. It wasn't easy, turning in a test match-winning bowling performance when half your team were attached to drips.

He sent the two nurses down to the boundary, one to catch and one to wake up silly mid-off who had fallen asleep and was dribbling onto his pillow.

He ran in to bowl.

And stopped.

There was something moving behind the batsman. On TV the bowlers always stopped when something was moving behind the batsman.

On TV it was rarely a matron.

The nurses leapt into action when they saw matron. They shooed Luke back into bed, snatched the cricket cap off Mrs Burridge's bandaged head, and gathered up the pile of bedpans that had been the wicket.

'It's OK, it's a soft ball,' said Colin, going over to matron and showing her. 'We're allowed to play with it indoors at home.'

Matron, hands on hips, ignored him and continued to glare at the nurses.

'Did you see Luke's six?' Colin said to Mum and Dad, who were standing behind her. 'I wasn't bowling my best but it was still a good hit. Reckon he must be almost better, eh?'

He waited for them to look happy about this, and say how pleased they were that he'd brought the bat and ball in so Luke could get back to playing cricket instead of weaving baskets and making ashtrays out of bottle tops and all that boring stuff you have to do in hospital.

They didn't. They stood staring across the ward at Luke and their faces were so pale and unhappy that for a moment Colin thought they'd got gastric too.

Colin sat on the hard vinyl chair in the matron's office and watched Mum and Dad standing by the bed talking to Luke.

It was too far away to hear what they were saying but they were smiling, sort of, and touching him a lot. It didn't look as though there was much telling off going on.

In the nurses' room there was a lot of telling off going on. Matron's voice had been raised ever since she'd led the two nurses in there and slammed the door.

Even above the noisy air-conditioner rattling in

matron's wall, Colin could hear the odd word. 'Irresponsible' had been used several times and 'very sick'.

She must be telling them she's very sick and tired of them being irresponsible, thought Colin.

He started writing a letter to matron in his head in case she gave the nurses the sack and he had to get their jobs back.

'Dear Matron, Overseas, where they have the best hospitals in the world, cricket is often used to help patients get better. Spin bowling is good exercise for people who've done their wrists in and batting is specially good for gastric because it strengthens the bowel muscles . . .'

Dad came into the matron's office and closed the door behind him. He still looked pale and unhappy. Colin waited for a telling off.

Instead Dad put his hands on Colin's shoulders.

'The hospital in Sydney that did the tests on Luke's blood want to do some more,' he said in a strange, low voice. 'Luke has to go down there, today.'

Probably so they can check out his poos, thought Colin. Boy, those Sydney hospitals are thorough all right.

'Are we all going in the car?' he asked.

'That'd take too long,' said Dad. 'They're flying him down in the air-ambulance this afternoon.'

Colin felt the blood drain from his face.

'There's only room for one passenger in the plane so I'm going with him,' said Dad. 'You and Mum'll come down on the train tomorrow.'

He crouched down in front of Colin and looked into his face. 'I know it's a shock, old mate, but we've got to be tough, eh?'

Colin barely heard him. His blood was pounding in his ears and he felt sick in the stomach.

It was a shock all right. A plane. He'd never even been in an ambulance and Luke was flying to Sydney in a plane.

'You ever had a crash?' Colin asked the air-ambulance pilot.

'Nope,' said the air-ambulance pilot, biting into his baked bean and salad sandwich.

Colin squinted out over the dusty airstrip. Gusts of hot wind were whipping up spirals of dirt and flinging them against the side of the little white plane.

'Probably be a bumpy flight,' said Colin.

'Yep,' said the pilot, taking a mouthful of chocolate-flavoured milk.

'Probably be a bit harder to navigate than usual,' said Colin.

The pilot shrugged.

'I'm pretty good at reading maps,' said Colin.

The pilot took another bite of his sandwich and another swig of his drink and chewed it all up together.

'And I've got a compass so we wouldn't wander round in circles gradually getting weaker and weaker until we perished from thirst if we did crash,' said Colin.

The pilot swallowed the last of his chocolate milk, burped, and stood up.

'Sorry,' he said, 'we're full up.'

He walked out of the tiny terminal and over towards the plane. Colin watched him go, then went over to where Dad was sitting, elbows on his knees, squeezing his hands together.

'Pilot reckons it'll probably be a bumpy flight.'

'Probably will,' said Dad, not looking up from his white knuckles.

'If you're feeling a bit nervous about it, I'll go,' said Colin.

Before Dad could answer, the ambulance from the hospital arrived and Dad jumped up and went out to meet it. Colin followed him, wishing that Luke would fall out of the ambulance and need micro-surgery on his neck so at least there'd be a reason for flying him around in planes at the taxpayer's expense.

Mum got out of the ambulance first, looking even tenser than Dad. Not surprising, thought Colin. Being stuck in there with Luke rabbiting on about how excited he was and whether they'd be attacked by MiGs on the way to Sydney would make anyone tense.

Then the ambulance men wheeled Luke out and Colin suddenly felt strange.

Luke wasn't rabbiting on about anything. He was just lying on the stretcher looking pale and sad. He looked up at Colin and spoke in a tiny voice.

'See ya, Col.'

'See ya, Luke,' said Colin and suddenly it was swirlier inside his chest than it was out on the airstrip.

A horrible thought snuck up on him. What if it's something worse than gastric? Something really crook like glandular fever or hepatitis?

Just for a second Colin's guts went cold, like when he remembered he hadn't done his homework, only worse. Then he did what he usually did with homework.

He stopped thinking about it.

Mum hugged Luke and Dad and then Luke was being wheeled across the the bumpy dirt towards the plane. Dad started to follow, then turned back and crouched down in front of Colin.

'Look after Mum for me, old mate,' he said and squeezed Colin's shoulder and was gone.

Colin moved closer to Mum, who had wet cheeks and was pressing her lips together very hard.

Colin watched the little plane soar into the hot sky, and once it was safely up he turned away. OK for kids, he thought, all that flying stuff, when you haven't got responsibilities.

He took Mum by the hand.

Chapter Four

'Looks very nice,' said Mum, poking the green lumps on her plate. 'What exactly is it?'

'Curry,' said Colin.

'Why's it green?'

'Well,' said Colin, 'the sausages burnt a bit while the rice was boiling over so I put some peas in.'

'Ah,' said Mum. She put a green lump into her mouth and chewed slowly.

Colin watched anxiously.

'Like it?'

He'd already tasted it himself and it wasn't bad though it could have done with a few less glacé cherries.

Mum swallowed and gave him a strange little smile.

'Very nice, love.'

She hates it, he thought. Right, that's it, I'm never putting dried fruit in a curry ever again.

'I like the cherries,' she said.

It's the onions, he thought, I knew I should have chopped them up.

Mum put her knife and fork down and took a deep

breath. Oh no, he thought, I didn't get all those lumps of curry powder out.

He had a vision of what Dad would say when he heard. 'I asked you to look after her for me, you drop-kick, not poison her.'

He grabbed a glass, filled it with water and pressed it into her hand. She seemed not to notice. It couldn't be the curry powder.

'Colin,' she said, 'there's something we haven't told you about Luke. The reason they've sent him to Sydney is cause they think he might be pretty crook.'

I don't believe it, thought Colin. I've just spent ages slaving in the kitchen cooking tea and now it's getting cold while she rabbits on about Luke.

'Mum,' he said, 'you've seen those Sydney hospitals on telly. They're huge. They've got equipment down there that can cure a horse.'

Mum looked at him for a moment, then smiled wearily. 'Good on you, Colin. You're right. No point in moping till we know what's what.'

'Now stop worrying,' said Colin, 'and eat your tea.'

He watched her lift a green lump on the end of her fork, look at it and put it back down.

'Sorry, love, I'm just not hungry.'

Colin's heart sank.

Then the phone rang.

Mum rushed into the hall and answered it in her long-distance voice. It was Dad, ringing from the Sydney hospital to say that Luke had just been taken away for his tests and to see how she and Colin were.

'I'm fine,' yelled Mum. 'Colin's just cooked me a wonderful tea and I feel awful cause I've lost my appetite.'

In the kitchen, Colin, who was about to scrape the curry off Mum's plate into the garbage, grinned and put the plate into the fridge instead.

Colin had a busy evening.

While Mum packed her bag for Sydney, Colin told her about a documentary he'd seen on TV where a man whose heart had gone bung had someone else's heart fitted into his chest. And another bloke who'd chopped his foot off with the lawnmower had it sewn back on. And a kid who'd swallowed several bits of her dad's record player had her tummy cut open and inside they found all the bits and a torch key-ring.

Then he heard Mr O'Brien's dog in the porch chewing the front door mat and he went out and threw some lumps of wood at it, just like Dad did most nights, and stood with his hands on his hips watching it run across the street to rub its bottom on Mrs Widdup's chook-wire fence.

Best of all was when Mum jammed her finger in the zipper of her suitcase. Colin put some Dettol on it and a Band-aid.

'It'll sting for a bit,' he told her.

'It already is,' she said.

'I like the smell of Dettol,' he said, to take her mind off it.

'Me included,' she said.

She let him stay up with her to watch the late news.

There was a story from England about two little kids born joined together who'd just been separated in a successful operation which, Colin thought, must have been a great relief for both of them.

Then he did his packing, just a couple of things in his cricket bag because they'd all be coming home on the train in a few days. Unless Luke had a very rare type of gastric which Channel Nine wanted to make a TV show about and Luke had to stay in Sydney for a couple of years.

Colin went to sleep thinking about that and slept soundly except for a couple of times when the phone rang outside his room and he could vaguely hear shouting, which might have been Mum or it might have been a TV producer telling Luke to relax and act natural.

He opened his eyes and it was still dark.

Somebody was squeezing into bed next to him. For a second he thought it was Luke, sneaking in with wet pyjama pants like he did last year after he'd turned his own bed into a one-boy irrigation area.

Then he realised it was Mum.

She pressed against him and she was wet too, on her cheek.

'Mum?' he whispered.

'Do you mind?' she said.

'Course not,' he replied.

Must be her finger, he thought. They can hurt a lot at night, fingers.

When he opened his eyes again it was morning and the big holiday suitcase was open on his bedroom floor.

The holiday suitcase?

Then he saw that inside it were just about all of his clothes.

He sat up.

Mum was sitting on the end of the bed looking at him.

'Colin,' she said softly, in a voice he'd never heard her use before, 'me and Dad'd like you to go and stay with Uncle Bob and Aunty Iris in England.'

Colin stared at her.

'We're not going to make you go,' she continued, 'but we'd like you to go. For you and for us.'

Words and questions and panic flew around in Colin's head but all he could say was . . .

'Why?'

Mum looked away. 'You'll have a great time over there. Uncle Bob and Aunty Iris live near the zoo and Uncle Bob goes to the cricket all the time. And your cousin Alistair's virtually your age.'

Colin's chest was pounding like a bore-pump.

They were sending him away.

They didn't want him any more.

'I can't go,' he said. 'I'm in the middle of a science project. Cricket practice starts next week . . .'

Mum moved up the bed and hugged him to her

and he could feel sobs booming around inside her chest. She took several deep breaths.

'The doctors say Luke isn't going to get better,' she said. 'They showed Dad the x-rays.'

X-rays? For gastric?

'I can help you,' he shouted. 'Make tea so you and Dad can look after him, bring his homework home from school, you don't have to send me away.'

'Colin,' said Mum, 'a terrible thing's happening and we don't want you to have to suffer too.'

What could be more terrible than sending him away?

'Don't you understand?' said Mum, and it was almost as if she was pleading with him. 'Luke's going to die.'

Colin sat on the roof of the shed and stared out over the paddocks. The sun-scorched corrugated iron stung his legs and he didn't care.

How dare they, he thought. How dare they give up and let Luke die.

Did they expect him to believe that they could take a bloke's heart out and put another one in and sew a foot back on and pull a torch key-ring out of a girl's stomach and yet they couldn't cure his brother of cancer?

Bull.

What about the man in the newsagent's? He'd had cancer on the head and they'd cured him.

In the far distance he could see a tiny machine stirring up a huge cloud of dust.

Did they expect him to believe that modern technology could bring the cricket live from India and make bombs that could blow up the whole world and build a combine harvester like Ian Pearce's dad's over there, with air-conditioning and built-in stereo headphones, and yet it couldn't stop Luke dying?

Bull.

They had millions of dollars worth of modern technology down there in those Sydney hospitals, he'd seen it on TV.

It was the doctors.

They weren't trying hard enough. The automatic aerials on their cars were probably playing up and they couldn't concentrate on work.

He thought for a while about going down to Sydney and telling them to pull their fingers out. Then it occurred to him that perhaps the Sydney doctors just weren't good enough.

What Luke needed was the best doctor in the world.

I'm going to need some help on this one, thought Colin, someone important who knows the phone number of the world's best doctor.

He thought a bit more.

Then he went to tell Mum he was going to England.

Chapter Five

On the train to Sydney, Colin tried to tell Mum about his plan.

'You don't have to worry,' he said, 'everything's going to be OK.'

She was staring out the window at the Wheat Board silo, the one Luke always said was a secret fuel dump for MiGs, and dabbing her eyes.

'Luke isn't going to die,' said Colin.

He was about to tell her the details of his plan when he realised she was still staring out the window.

'Mum, I said Luke isn't going to die.'

She turned to him sharply.

'Don't talk about things you don't understand,' she said in a loud whisper.

Colin saw her glance at the other people in the carriage, who had been looking at them with interest. The other people suddenly became even more interested in the black and white photo of the Lithgow suspension bridge screwed to the wall over Colin's head.

'I do understand,' said Colin.

'Love,' she said in a softer voice, 'it's not up to us.'

'I know,' said Colin, 'that's what I'm trying to explain.'

'Look, why don't you think about all the exciting things you're going to be doing with Uncle Bob and Aunty Iris and Alistair?'

Stack me, thought Colin, some people don't want to be cheered up.

'Mum, I'm trying to tell you about Luke.'

Suddenly he found himself being pressed to her shirt, her quivering arms locked tight round him.

'Don't talk about it,' he heard her sob into the top of his head, 'please don't.'

All right, he thought, I won't.

At the hospital in Sydney he tried to tell Dad about Luke not dying and Dad asked him not to as well.

'We've got to be strong, old mate, and cop it on the chin,' he said, his voice shaking.

Colin looked at his father's red, bloodshot eyes and wondered why nobody wanted to hear the good news.

Mum and Dad stopped him as he was about to go into Luke's room.

'Don't say anything to Luke, old mate, about . . . you know,' said Dad. 'The doctors haven't and we've decided not to.'

'Don't worry, I won't,' said Colin.

Say what, thought Colin, that he's going to die? Well I wouldn't say that, would I, cause he's not.

As it turned out, Colin didn't have a chance to say

anything. Luke was asleep, his small figure completely surrounded by quivering dials and flickering gauges and blinking lights and glowing screens.

He looks like he's flying a MiG, thought Colin. The electricity that must be going into that lot. He'd remind Dad of that next time Dad yelled at him to turn a light off.

The international airport was full of people bawling their eyes out.

Colin watched them throwing their arms round each other and making damp patches on each other's clothes.

Perhaps grown-ups like crying, he thought. That would explain Mum and Dad's behaviour, and why so many people fly overseas. Adults aren't allowed to cry when they fall off a bike or hit their thumb with a hammer, but they can howl like five year olds when they've got a duty free bag in their hands.

'. . . be a good boy for Uncle Bob and Aunty Iris,' Mum was saying through her tears, 'and have a wonderful time. We'll be thinking of you.'

No you won't, thought Colin, you'll be thinking about Luke, as well as being with him night and day, and playing with him, and buying him things, and spoiling him rotten.

Until I get back that is.

Colin saw himself arriving back in the best doctor in the world's private Lear jet, being whisked by helicopter to the hospital, where the best doctor in the world would operate immediately, Luke would be cured, and Mum and Dad would spend the rest of their lives trying to express their gratitude to Colin, probably starting with a small statue in the front yard.

'. . . and be sure to thank Uncle Bob and Aunty Iris very very much for having you,' Mum was saying, 'and give them our love. This is for you.'

Colin looked down and saw that she'd pushed into his hand three strange-looking brown banknotes.

'English money,' said Mum. 'It's not much I'm afraid, but we didn't have much left after buying your air ticket.'

'Don't worry,' said Colin, 'I won't need much.'

Mum folded the money up and tucked it into the plastic wallet with his air ticket and the passport they'd spent the last two days rushing around Sydney getting.

'This is the best way,' said Mum, starting to cry again. 'Once you're over there it won't be so painful for you and we'll send for you when it's all. . . when it's all . . .'

Colin watched her trying to say 'over'. He was about to grab her and yell 'watch my lips' and tell her that Luke wasn't going to die when Dad arrived with the Qantas lady.

During the flight Colin worked out the details of his plan.

The flight attendants were very nice to him, bringing him meals before anyone else and asking him every half an hour if he wanted another orange juice and listening patiently to his suggestions about improving the plane.

Colin told them that if they moved all the seats over a bit there'd be room down one side for a really good in-flight cricket pitch. They nodded thoughtfully and said they'd pass that on to the captain.

The businessman sitting next to Colin didn't seem so friendly. Over Indonesia he cleared his throat and Colin thought he was going to say something, but he went back to reading his magazine.

Over India he went to the toilet. As he sat back down in his seat he gave a grunt of pain.

Colin decided that with another eleven and a half hours to go, he should probably start a conversation.

The businessman shifted in his seat and gave another grunt of pain.

'Is that a bit of cancer?' asked Colin.

The businessman stared at him.

'I beg your pardon?'

'Cancer,' said Colin, 'it's where cells start growing too fast inside your body and your whole system can go bung.'

'I know what it is,' snapped the businessman, 'I just don't particularly want to talk about it.'

'Why not?' asked Colin.

'Because it's not a very pleasant topic,' said the businessman, sounding just like Mr Blair when Arnie Strachan asked why sick had bits in it.

'If you've got it I'd get it seen to,' said Colin.

'I haven't got it,' snapped the businessman, wriggling in his seat. 'I've got indigestion.'

'Mum's always warning us about getting that,' said Colin. 'Did you go out and climb a tree straight after a meal?'

The businessman didn't answer. He closed his eyes and pretended to go to sleep.

Indigestion, thought Colin. Maybe Luke's just got indigestion.

No, he thought, even doctors with the most serious car problem in the world, like dropping the keys down the toilet and not knowing which toilet, wouldn't make a mistake like that.

Over Yugoslavia the whole plane was asleep except for Colin, who was deep in thought.

'Dear Luke,' he wrote in his head, 'flight over was very pleasant with free lemonade, orange juice and Coke. Did you have a choice of drinks on the air-ambulance? Probably not, as you don't get the same standard of service on the smaller airlines . . .'

He was interrupted by a flight attendant tapping him on the shoulder and asking him if he'd like to go up front and meet the captain.

Must want to talk about the in-flight cricket pitch, thought Colin as he followed the attendant towards the front of the plane.

On the flight deck were more dials, gauges, knobs, switches, levers and screens than Colin had ever seen in one place before. The whole cabin pulsed with the quiet throb of incredibly complicated machinery.

'So,' said the captain shaking hands with Colin, 'we're travelling to London by ourselves.'

No we're not, thought Colin, looking at the other uniformed men sitting in the cabin.

'Yes, I am,' he said.

'What are you going to do in London?' asked the captain. 'British Museum? Trafalgar Square? Ride in a red bus?'

'Buckingham Palace,' said Colin.

'Ah,' said the captain. 'Changing of the Guard, eh?'

'No,' said Colin, 'I'm going to see the Queen.'

The other men in the cabin grinned at each other.

'See the Queen?' said the captain, winking at one of them. 'Going to drop in for tea are you?'

'No,' said Colin. 'I'm going to ask her to help cure my brother's cancer.'

In the long silence that followed, Colin took a closer look at the equipment humming and blinking all around him.

If modern technology could do this, he thought, keep a plane bigger than Bayliss's Department Store up in the air sixty thousand feet over Dubrovnik, it could cure cancer standing on its head.

Chapter Six

Will I tell them or won't I, wondered Colin as he wheeled his luggage trolley down the airport corridor behind the London Qantas lady.

He tested out telling them in his head. 'Nice to meet you Uncle Bob and Aunty Iris but I've really come to London to see the Queen.'

'Oh, is that right, young man? Well if our hot meals and spare bed aren't good enough for you, you can rack off.'

He followed the London Qantas lady out into the Heathrow Arrivals Hall. Thousands of English faces peered at him to see if he was their cousin from Buenos Aires or their uncle from Karachi.

It'd be an easier decision to make if he'd met Uncle Bob and Aunty Iris before, but he'd only seen a photo and that'd had a fly spot on it.

What if they turned out to be good friends of the Queen? He knew Uncle Bob worked for the local council. Perhaps the Queen dropped by sometimes to see how the roadworks were going. If he didn't tell them, they might never say.

He still hadn't decided what to do when he saw Aunty Iris lunging towards him, arms outstretched.

And there was Uncle Bob behind her. He didn't look much like Mum's brother. For a start her mouth curved up at the corners and his curved down.

Next to Uncle Bob was the whitest kid Colin had ever seen. And huge. Colin was sure Mum had said cousin Alistair was only thirteen but he was built like a brick dunny and was taller than Uncle Bob.

After the hugging and kissing and shaking hands and questions about Mum and Dad and the food on the plane, they all stood looking at each other.

Except for Aunty Iris, who was looking at Alistair.

'Don't stand like that, love, you'll damage your spine.'

Alistair straightened up half a millimetre.

'You heard what your mother said,' said Uncle Bob. 'I'm not paying for you to have your posture straightened.'

'Sorry,' said Alistair.

'Well,' said Aunty Iris, smiling, 'we might as well be off then.'

'Less time in that car-park the better,' said Uncle Bob. 'It's a disgrace, charging like that to park a car.'

Colin noticed the large mole next to Uncle Bob's nose. It hadn't been a flyspot on the photo after all.

They moved off towards the car-park.

No one had mentioned Luke.

Colin huddled into the back seat of the little car as it sped along the motorway. He'd never been so cold, and that was with the car heater on.

In the airport car-park the cold had hit him like a kick in the guts and sent him burrowing inside his suitcase for more clothes.

'There's Windsor Castle,' said Aunty Iris, pointing.

Uncle Bob gave a snort and put his foot down.

Colin turned round to look. It wasn't easy as he was wearing all four of the jumpers he'd brought with him.

Through the rain-spattered car window all he could see was fog. Then a big truck roared past and sprayed the window with dirty, half-melted slush and he couldn't even see the fog.

'Are you hoping to see some of the sights while you're here?' asked Aunty Iris. 'Alistair, don't pick your scalp, you'll get scabs.'

Colin decided to risk it.

'I want to go to Buckingham Palace,' he said.

Uncle Bob gave another snort.

'Why would you want to go to that dump?' he demanded, glaring at Colin in the rear-vision mirror. 'Waste of taxpayers money, that place. Ought to be pulled down. Alistair, you heard what your mother said.'

Colin was shocked. Buckingham Palace hadn't looked like a dump on Mrs Widdup's place mat. Though it had been a fairly old place mat. Perhaps they'd had problems recently, termites or something.

'I'm not really that interested in the palace,' he said. 'It's the Queen I want to see.'

Colin saw Aunty Iris flinch slightly.

'Don't talk to me about the Queen,' growled Uncle Bob. 'You get me started on the Queen . . .'

'All right, Bob,' said Aunty Iris hastily, 'you mind the road.' She turned to Colin. 'Don't mind Uncle Bob, he's got a bit of a thing about the Royal Family.'

'Thinks they should be stuffed and put in a museum,' said Alistair.

'All right, Alistair,' said Aunty Iris. 'Is your seat belt done up tight enough?' She gave it a tug, then turned back to Colin.

'Anyway,' she continued, 'we don't go into the city as a rule. Can't hear yourself think in there. But don't worry, we'll be able to show you all the sights. Got them all in a lovely big book at home. What else are you planning to do while you're here?'

Colin decided not to tell them.

After another hour of driving through slush, fog and heavy traffic, they arrived in Uncle Bob and Aunty Iris's suburb.

'If you're not too tired,' said Aunty Iris, 'we thought we might have a bit of an afternoon out.'

'Take your mind off other things,' said Alistair.

'Just a bit of fun and relaxation,' said Aunty Iris, glaring at Alistair. She smiled at Colin. 'Do you good to relax after that long flight and . . . and . . .'

'Other things,' said Uncle Bob.

He swung the wheel and they turned into a huge car park in front of what looked to Colin like a massive warehouse. It certainly wasn't Buckingham Palace.

'No,' said Colin wearily, 'I'm not tired.'

They got out of the car.

Still no mention of Luke.

'This,' said Uncle Bob proudly, 'is the biggest Do-It-Yourself Hardware Centre in Greater London.'

Colin looked around. There was a lot of hardware.

The massive warehouse building was full of it. Giant supermarket aisles stretched away as far as the eye could see, and on every shelf, hook, and rack, and in every basket, tub and storage unit, was hardware.

'Pretty incredible, isn't it?' said Uncle Bob.

'What do you think?' said Aunty Iris. 'Alistair, don't play with the saws.'

I don't believe it, thought Colin. I've just flown half-way round the world to save my brother's life and here I am staring at pre-painted bathroom panels.

'It's bigger than ours at home,' he said.

Uncle Bob, Aunty Iris and Alistair laughed the laugh of people who had just heard what they wanted to hear.

'We were a bit worried when they first built it,' said Uncle Bob, 'but it's the focal point of the district now.'

'We're very pleased with it,' said Aunty Iris. 'Alistair, don't touch that.'

'Do you mind if we go now?' said Colin. 'I'm actually finding it a bit hard to concentrate on hardware while Luke's got cancer.'

The silence that followed lasted long enough for Alistair to cut his finger on a wallpaper scraper.

By the time they had been to the hospital and waited to have Alistair's finger looked at, and Uncle Bob had had an argument with the medical supervisor about wasting the hospital's time, and Colin had asked the medical supervisor if he knew anything about cancer, and the medical supervisor had thought Colin was being sarcastic and had ordered them all off the premises, it was teatime.

After tea, Aunty Iris thought Alistair was looking pale and sent him to bed early.

Colin said he needed an early night too. He lay on the lumpy bed in the spare room and stared at the ceiling. He wondered what the Queen was doing. Working on next year's Christmas speech perhaps. Perhaps it had given her a headache and even at that moment the best doctor in the world was being rushed across London in a police motorcade.

He wondered how quickly cancer made the body go bung. He couldn't afford to waste any more time. He had to see her tomorrow. But first he needed some information.

He crept into Alistair's room. Alistair was in bed, reading a Captain America comic. On the cover Captain America was fighting about fifty slime-covered reptiles. Alistair guiltily stuffed it under his pillow until he saw it was only Colin.

'Alistair,' said Colin, 'where exactly is Buckingham Palace?'

'In town,' said Alistair. 'Miles away.'

'How do you get there?'

'Quickest way's by tube,' said Alistair, 'but it's pretty dangerous. You have to get into the same carriage as dozens of other people. You can catch a cold or flu or anything. Well, not anything. A lot of things but not, you know, anything.'

'It's OK, Alistair,' said Colin. 'I know you don't catch cancer from other people.'

Alistair looked pained.

'Mum said that word isn't to be mentioned in this house while you're here.'

'What word?'

'That word.'

'Cancer?'

'Shhhh.'

Colin looked at Alistair and the thought occurred to him that perhaps being an only child wasn't all it was cracked up to be.

Downstairs the phone rang.

'Quickly,' Aunty Iris called up. 'It's your mum and dad.'

Colin raced down.

'I've told them you arrived OK,' said Aunty Iris.

Mum and Dad sounded very faint. Colin wasn't sure if it was because they were very far away or because they were very unhappy.

'Don't worry,' he shouted into the phone, 'everything's going to be OK.'

There was an echo on the line and he heard his own voice.

'. . . going to be OK.'

Chapter Seven

Next morning it was still dark when Colin woke. Perfect, he thought. Best to make an early start when you're going to see the Queen. You'd kick yourself if you got there late and she'd gone shopping or something.

He dressed quickly, wrote a short note ('Gone for a walk. Cricket training. Back later') and crept down the stairs, hoping to slip out of the house before anyone else was up.

No such luck.

'Morning, Colin,' said Uncle Bob, looking over the top of his newspaper.

'Morning, Colin,' said Aunty Iris, coming out of the kitchen with a tray of breakfast things.

'Morning, Colin,' said Alistair, sitting at the dining-table with a mouthful of bacon.

'G'day,' said Colin, pushing the note into his pocket. 'What time is it?'

His watch said six-thirty but it had been running a bit crook ever since Arnie Strachan dropped it in a pineapple yoghurt.

'Eight-fourteen,' said Uncle Bob.

'Why's it so dark outside?' asked Colin.

'Don't talk to me about dark,' said Uncle Bob. 'This country's like a coal-mine in winter.'

'You slept well,' said Aunty Iris. 'Alistair, chew your food.'

Colin looked out the window and saw that it was just getting light. He'd have to hurry.

''Fraid we're going to have to leave you on your own today,' said Aunty Iris. 'Alistair's coming to work with me so I can take him to the doctor's at lunchtime.'

'I'm sickening for something,' said Alistair, shovelling a whole fried egg into his mouth.

'We want you to make yourself right at home,' said Aunty Iris. 'There's the telly and the wireless and Uncle Bob's Do-It-Yourself magazines. The important thing is, relax and take your mind completely off, you know, things.'

'Thanks,' said Colin. 'I've got heaps to keep me occupied.'

Colin rubbed a peep-hole in the misted-up front room window and watched the little car chug away in a cloud of white exhaust.

He counted to ten.

Then he ran upstairs, hauled on his other three jumpers, slammed the front door behind him and sprinted down the street.

He'd seen the underground station as they'd approached the house the evening before and he didn't stop running till he'd reached it. He hurried down the steps, lungs raw in the icy air, and bought a ticket and a map of London.

The train arrived and it was as crowded as Alistair had said, hundreds of people jammed into every carriage. Colin squeezed in and felt the sliding doors brush his shoulders as they closed behind him.

At the next station even more people crushed in, and more at the next. Colin's feet were barely touching the ground. An umbrella was sticking in his ear.

He thought of Mum and Dad and Luke, tucked up in their beds in Australia, and wished they knew what he was going through so they could appreciate it.

Then he realised he didn't know which station he had to get off at for Buckingham Palace.

'S'cuse me,' he said to the twenty people nearest to him, 'which station do I get off at for Buckingham Palace?'

No one answered. No one even looked at him.

Perhaps they're all French tourists, he thought.

He said it again, louder. The twenty people nearest to him all stared intently into space. Which wasn't easy as the only space on the train was up near the ceiling.

Colin decided to look at his map.

Three stations later he'd managed to get it out of his pocket.

He was just wondering if taking some of his jumpers off would make enough space to fold it out when the train stopped at the next station. The doors slid open and everyone got off at once.

Colin was swept off with them and carried along the platform in a tidal wave of bodies and up an escalator and past the ticket collector and out into the street.

The city roared all around him. He got his breath back and folded out the map.

A black man with a yellow beanie stopped and looked over Colin's shoulder.

'Where you going to?' he asked.

'To see the Queen,' said Colin.

The man grinned and pointed up the street. 'Give the old girl my regards,' he said.

That's good, thought Colin as he walked along the street, at least she's approachable.

It was the biggest house he'd ever seen.

There must be hundreds of rooms in there, he thought, staring up at the rows and rows of windows. And twenty or thirty toilets.

Folks at home'd call it a palace, thought Colin, and they'd be right. The front yard alone was as big as a footy pitch, and all gravel.

Colin was impressed. Mrs Widdup had had her front yard gravelled, and even the cost of that little bit had meant she hadn't been able to afford a front fence. She'd had to put up chicken wire.

The Queen hadn't had that problem. Her front fence was black and iron and three times as high as Colin with gold spikes on top.

Her front gate was bigger than Colin's house.

And shut tight.

Colin looked around for a bell.

There wasn't one.

Then he noticed a large group of tourists nearby. They were taking photos of a guard in a red tunic and a big black furry helmet.

Colin pushed his way through the throng.

''Scuse me,' he said to the guard, 'I'm here to see the Queen.'

The guard didn't move a muscle.

Colin couldn't understand it. This one definitely couldn't be a French tourist.

Colin said it again, louder.

The guard didn't even look at him.

'Hey,' yelled a French tourist to Colin, 'you are in my picture.'

'Please tell the Queen that Colin Mudford is here from Australia,' said Colin to the guard.

A Spanish tourist stepped forward grinning.

'And Manuel Corbes from Madrid,' he said.

Colin and the guard both ignored him.

'I need the Queen's help,' said Colin to the guard.

The guard ignored Colin as well. Colin moved round so he was directly in front of the guard's unblinking gaze.

'It's an urgent medical matter,' said Colin, speaking slowly and trying to move his lips so that if the guard was deaf he could lip-read.

'My . . . brother . . . Luke . . . has . . . got . . . cancer.'

'My brother's got dandruff,' said an American

tourist loudly, 'but that don't mean I go round messing up other folks' photo opportunities.'

Colin felt himself beginning to get angry.

'Look,' he said to the guard, 'just let me in and I'll explain inside.'

'Me too,' said the Spanish tourist. His friends laughed.

The guard was as motionless as the stone lion on the gatepost behind him.

Colin controlled himself.

'Look,' he said, 'I know you're probably not meant to open the gate and you probably get people lying through their teeth all the time, but I promise you I'm telling the truth and if you open the gate I'll explain everything to the Queen and you won't lose your job or get sent to Northern Ireland.'

The gate stayed shut.

Colin lost his temper.

'You'd better open that gate,' he yelled at the guard, 'cause when the Queen finds out you've kept a kid with cancer waiting she's gunna do you.'

A hand dropped on to Colin's shoulder.

He spun round and found himself face to face with the shiny buttons of a policeman.

'All right,' said the policeman, 'break it up. Come on, move along. You lot are never satisfied. We put a guardsman out here to stop you sticking your cameras through the railings and dropping them and what thanks do we get? Go on, you've had your lot for today.'

The tourists wandered away muttering and glaring at Colin.

'Right, son,' said the policeman, 'what's your problem?'

'I need to see the Queen about my sick brother,' said Colin.

The policeman gave a hollow laugh.

'Oh really. Well I suggest you ring her up and have a chat about it. If I see you hanging around here again you'll be the one who's feeling sick.'

The first phone box didn't have a phone.

The second one had a phone but no receiver.

The third one had a phone and a receiver but all that was left of the phone books was a pile of ash on the floor and the coin slot was clogged up with bubblegum.

Colin looked at it and felt like crying.

It had taken him an hour to find these three phone boxes. He'd walked miles, he had a headache from the roaring traffic and his mouth tasted as though he'd been sucking an exhaust pipe.

He didn't cry.

Instead he crossed the road to a large and very posh hotel. He went up to a large and very posh doorman in a green and gold uniform.

'Can I use your phone, please?' he said.

'Are you a guest at this hotel, sir?' asked the doorman, glancing down at Colin's elastic-sided boots. One of them was even more scuffed than usual where he'd kicked the third phone box.

'Look,' said Colin, 'I'll give you ten pounds if I can use your phone.'

He held out one of Mum's brown ten pound notes.

The doorman took the ten pounds, folded it up very small, tucked it firmly into Colin's shirt pocket, and directed him to a phone box that worked in a quiet street round the corner.

Colin ran to the box and pulled the door open. There was a phone. With a receiver. And phone books. He started hunting through them.

Q for Queen.

Nothing.

P for Palace.

Nothing.

R for Royal Family.

Nothing.

B for Buckingham.

Someone had torn out all the pages up to Carruthers.

He rang the operator.

'Have you got a number for the Queen, please?' he asked.

The operator hung up.

Colin went out and bought a can of lemonade and asked for the change (nine pounds 30p) in 10p pieces.

Then he rang The City of London Information Centre, The Houses of Parliament, The Home Office, The Times, The London Transport Information Centre and Harrods.

Nobody would tell him the Queen's telephone number.

He carried on ringing.

The Victoria and Albert Museum, The Royal Albert Hall, The Royal Festival Hall, The Royal Opera House Covent Garden and The Royale Fish Bar, Peckham.

The man in the Royale Fish Bar gave him the number of a man who used to deliver fish to Buckingham Palace.

The man who used to deliver fish to Buckingham Palace gave him the number of the man in charge of catering at Buckingham Palace.

The man in charge of catering at Buckingham Palace gave him the number of the Public Relations Office at Buckingham Palace.

Colin dialled the number.

He asked the man who answered if the Queen could come to the phone and the man said that all communications with the Palace had to be in writing and that trouble-makers would be prosecuted.

Then he hung up.

That night Colin helped Aunty Iris dry up the tea things and then sat down and wrote the Queen a letter.

Dear Your Majesty The Queen, he wrote.

I need to speak to you urgently about my brother Luke. He's got cancer and the doctors in Australia are being really slack. If I could borrow your top doctor for a few days I know he/she would fix things up in no time. Of course Mum and Dad would pay his/her fares even if it

meant selling the car or getting a loan. Please contact me at the above address urgently.
Yours sincerely,
Colin Mudford
PS *This is not a hoax. Ring the above number and Aunty Iris will tell you. Hang up if a man answers.*

He went out and posted it straight away.

Then he waited.

Chapter Eight

Three days later he was still waiting.

Sitting at the breakfast table he heard the postman pushing letters through the flap in the front door.

He raced out into the hall and scooped them up off the mat.

Gas bill, Reader's Digest, local church magazine, a small parcel from Birmingham that rattled . . .

Nothing from the Queen.

'Don't fret, love,' said Aunty Iris, taking the letters from him. 'You only left six days ago. Takes at least seven days for a letter to get here from Australia.'

'Don't talk to me about seven days,' muttered Uncle Bob from behind his newspaper. 'What about that Christmas card? Came via Israel.'

Aunty Iris gave Colin a little hug. 'Feeling a bit homesick, are you, pet? Give Mum and Dad a quick ring. Go on, we don't mind, just the once.'

'No, it's OK, I'm fine,' said Colin. 'Thanks, anyway.'

Part of him wanted to, desperately, but the other part didn't, not till he could tell them to whack the linseed oil on Luke's cricket bat, he was coming home with the world's best doctor.

Why hadn't the Queen replied?

She must have a writing pad. She must have to answer letters all the time.

Colin had a sudden vision of the front door at Buckingham Palace, letters pouring in through the flap and piling up in great mountains all down the hall, with a queue of postmen outside waiting to push sackfuls more in.

Of course. What a dill he'd been.

He'd have to see her in person.

Aunty Iris and Uncle Bob were putting their coats on for work.

'Alistair,' called Aunty Iris, 'those kelp tablets have come and they're on the bench in the kitchen. Take two every hour with water and if you go into the garden wrap up and no climbing. And I don't want you out near that traffic. Bye.'

The front door closed.

Colin looked at the marmalade jar in front of him on the table. By Royal Appointment to Her Majesty The Queen. What did he have to do to get to see her, become a marmalade manufacturer?

'Colin?' said Alistair.

For three days he'd been stuck in the house with Alistair, who wasn't allowed to do anything even remotely interesting in case he hurt himself. Even though the doctor had said that not only was Alistair not sickening for anything, he was the healthiest thirteen year old he'd ever seen apart from the dandruff.

Three days of questions about Australia.

'Have you really ridden a trail bike,' asked Alistair, 'or were you just pulling my leg?'

'Yamaha 250,' said Colin, 'twin exhaust, cross-country gear ratios.'

Alistair's eyes shone as he chewed his bacon.

'Must have been brilliant.'

'It was OK till the brakes failed and I went off a cliff.'

'A cliff?' Alistair stared at him in admiration.

Colin pulled himself together. This was what it had been like for three days, him exaggerating and Alistair wide-eyed with admiration and him exaggerating even more.

It had gone on long enough.

He looked at Alistair.

'Wanna help me save Luke's life?'

Alistair stared back, suddenly alarmed.

'What do you mean?' he stammered. 'I'm not allowed to give blood, Mum won't let me.'

Colin told him about the Queen and how he'd been trying to get to see her.

Alistair's eyes bulged.

Then Colin told him what he'd decided to do now.

If Aunty Iris had been there she would have told Alistair to put his eyes back into his head.

'What's all this got to do with me?' croaked Alistair.

'Simple,' said Colin. 'I need someone to give me a leg up.'

Buying the rope was simple enough once Colin had persuaded Alistair that it was OK to go to the shops.

'Mum doesn't like me going,' said Alistair, hanging around the front gate.

'What?' said Colin. 'Does she think a bus is going to mount the kerb, weave through all the other shoppers, carefully avoiding rubbish bins and brick walls, and flatten you?'

'Well, one could do, couldn't it?'

'OK,' said Colin, 'you stay here.'

'I'll come,' said Alistair.

The alarm went off under Colin's pillow and for a moment he thought Luke had borrowed Dad's electric drill again. His heart leaped. It had been bad enough the first time, Luke trying to repair the loose drawer in Colin's room and drilling through six pairs of underpants.

Colin opened his eyes and remembered where he was.

Then he remembered why he'd set the alarm.

He pulled the clock from under the pillow and peered at it in the darkness.

Three-thirty.

He got out of bed and got dressed as quickly as he could, which wasn't that quickly because his body was shivering all over and his fingers were going numb with the cold.

He felt under the bed and slid out his footy bag. He peered inside. The rope was still there. He pulled his top two jumpers up under his armpits, wound the rope round and round his middle, tied a knot, and pulled the jumpers back down over the rope.

Then he crept into Alistair's room and shook Alistair awake.

'I took the pills,' mumbled Alistair, 'honest, Mum.'

'It's time to go,' whispered Colin.

Alistair opened his eyes and blinked at Colin.

'I'm scared,' he said.

'Get dressed,' said Colin, 'or we'll miss the bus.'

'Mum doesn't let me go into town by myself,' said Alistair.

'You won't be by yourself,' said Colin. 'I'll be with you.'

'What if you get shot?'

'OK,' said Colin, 'you stay here.'

'I'll come,' said Alistair.

The driver of the night bus gave them a suspicious look as they got on and paid their fares.

Colin held his breath.

It was probably just that not many kids caught the 3.50am bus into town.

'It's a real pain having to start work at 4.30,' Colin said to Alistair. 'Still, that's the price we have to pay for owning our own milk bar.'

'Eh?' said Alistair.

The driver handed over the tickets and they hurried upstairs and sat at the back.

They travelled in silence for a few minutes, then Alistair turned to Colin.

'What if they've got dogs?' he said.

'They haven't got dogs,' said Colin.

'How do you know?'

'It was in our local paper at home,' said Colin. 'A couple of years ago a bloke got into Buckingham Palace at night and the next morning when the Queen woke up he was sitting on the end of her bed looking at her. He didn't have a single dog bite on him.'

'I remember that,' said Alistair.

'If he can do it, I can,' said Colin.

'They put him in a loony bin,' said Alistair.

Colin began to wish Alistair hadn't come.

They got off the bus in the middle of the freezing, empty city and Colin looked at his map under a streetlamp.

'What if we get lost?' said Alistair.

'We won't,' said Colin.

'It could take them days to find us,' said Alistair. 'We could starve. If we don't die from the pollution.'

'You don't have to come,' said Colin, crossing the road towards a park.

'I'll come,' said Alistair.

The park was black. They walked next to the railings for a long time.

'What if she wakes up and sees you sitting there and gets such a fright she wets the bed?' said Alistair suddenly. 'Do you know how many years in jail you'd get for making the Queen wet the bed?'

Colin sighed.

'I'm not gunna break into her bedroom, Dumbo,' he said. 'I'll wait in one of the toilets. When she's got up and had her breakfast I'll pop in the dining-room and have a word with her then.'

They turned a corner and there was the Palace.

Instead of the roaring traffic and milling tourists of three days ago, the huge space in front of the Palace was silent and empty.

Except for two policemen standing by the gate.

Alistair gave a little whimper.

Colin grabbed him and moved him along the railings, keeping out of the light from the streetlamps.

The policemen didn't look over.

Colin steered Alistair round a bend and there in front of them, stretching away as far as Colin could see, was the back wall of the Palace.

They crossed the road and stood at the base of the wall. It was three times as high as Colin and on the top were sharp black metal spikes.

'Don't let those spikes touch you,' said Alistair, trembling.

'I've got four jumpers on,' said Colin, lifting the top two and unwinding the rope from round his middle.

He tied a lasso knot in one end and while he was doing it, he suddenly remembered all the lasso knots he'd tied with Doug Beale those afternoons they'd spent lassoing Doug's younger sister Gaylene.

He looked up and down the road.

No cars.

No people.

He threw the lasso high up the wall. It hit a spike, slipped off and tumbled down.

'Hurry up,' hissed Alistair, trembling even more. 'Pretend it's one of those crocodiles you're always roping.'

Colin threw the lasso again and missed again. He wished he hadn't exaggerated about Gaylene.

He threw again.

The lasso flopped over a spike.

And stayed there.

Colin yanked it tight and hauled on the rope.

'OK,' he said to Alistair, 'give me a leg up.'

Alistair obviously hadn't given anybody a leg up before. It took him a while to grasp the concept. Then he started pushing Colin up the wall.

Colin could feel him trembling.

'Oh my God,' said Alistair.

Here we go, thought Colin, this is where he panics and we're history.

'Oh my God,' said Alistair again.

Colin glanced down at him, expecting to see a face white with panic. Instead he saw a face beaming with excitement.

'We're breaking into Buckingham Palace,' squeaked Alistair. 'Brilliant.'

He gave Colin an extra big heave and Colin started

to climb upwards, hand over hand on the rope, soles of his feet flat against the wall.

'Sodding brill,' piped up Alistair from below.

Colin didn't feel brill.

Fears started ballooning up inside him.

What if after the bloke had broken into her bedroom they'd got dogs?

Or mines?

Or a moat with sharks?

Or run electricity through the spikes?

The rope was cutting his hands and his back was nearly breaking. But he didn't stop. Because stronger than all the fear was the vision of him getting off the plane in Sydney with the world's best doctor, and the look on Mum and Dad's faces.

He climbed on, practising in his mind what he was going to say to the Queen. ('Sorry to barge in like this Your Majesty . . .')

He climbed on and on.

Until he was dazzled by a white and searing light.

Colin knew Uncle Bob and Aunty Iris would chuck a mental and they did.

They controlled themselves while the police lectured them on the sins of letting kids out at 3.30 at night and pointed out repeatedly to them how lucky everyone was that no one was being charged. This time.

But when the police had gone they really let rip.

'This is the thanks we get,' yelled Aunty Iris, 'for taking you into our home to give your mother and father a chance to cope with . . . things. Alistair, stop snivelling.'

'We're in the computer now,' roared Uncle Bob, 'this whole family, in the police computer. Alistair, use your hanky.'

'You could both have been killed,' yelled Aunty Iris. 'Specially you, Alistair. Well, that's it. You're both staying in the house from now on. I'll be locking the doors when I go to work and they'll stay locked till I get back.'

'That won't stop me,' yelled Colin. 'The Queen'll get to my letter eventually, then she'll come round here with a tank and bash the door down.'

'No she flippin' won't,' roared Uncle Bob.

You're right, thought Colin, she won't.

Afterwards, when the shouting had stopped and Colin was lying on his bed, he was surprised to see Uncle Bob's face appear round the door.

'Forget the Queen,' said Uncle Bob. 'The likes of her hasn't got time for the likes of us. In this world ordinary people have to solve their own problems.'

'I was just thinking that,' said Colin.

Chapter Nine

Colin started with the local doctor's surgery. He got the number from Alistair and dialled.

'G'day, could you tell me which is the best cancer hospital in London?'

'How old are you?' said a woman with a posh accent, which Colin could tell a mile off she was bunging on.

He told her.

'Sorry, we haven't got time for school projects,' she said and hung up.

Colin put another 10p into Aunty Iris's phone money tin and thought who to ring next.

The City of London Information Centre? The Houses of Parliament? The Times?

He rang the Royale Fish Bar in Peckham.

'Cancer 'ospital?' said the fish bar man, concerned. 'You poorly are you, son?'

'It's my brother,' said Colin.

'Poor bleeder,' said the man. ''Ang on, I'll ask the missus.'

He came back after a bit and said that the customers in the shop all agreed that the best cancer hospital in

London was the one that had cured Ernie Stringfellow's prostate trouble. He told Colin the name and the address.

'Hope it does the trick for 'im, son, God love 'im.'

Colin thanked the man, put the phone down and went out to the kitchen, where Alistair was trying to tie a lasso knot in his pyjama cord.

This was going to be the tricky bit.

Aunty Iris and Uncle Bob had locked both the front door and the back door and taken the keys to work with them. Ten seconds after they'd gone, Colin had checked all the downstairs windows and found that they'd got locks on them too.

He was a prisoner.

'Is there a screwdriver around?' asked Colin.

'Dad keeps all his tools out in the garage,' replied Alistair.

Colin had feared that.

'What do you want a screwdriver for?' asked Alistair.

'To take the lock off the back door.'

Alistair's eyes widened with horror.

'You can't do that. They'll go bananas. They'll kill us. You don't know my mum. She'll . . . they'll . . .'

Alistair was panicking.

Colin had feared that too.

'Listen,' he said, 'it's OK. I'll be back before they are and I'll put the lock back on and they'll never know.'

Alistair had stopped yelling and was just breathing heavily.

'Anyway,' he said, 'you can't take it off if you haven't got a screwdriver, can you?'

Colin went to the kitchen drawer and took out a knife.

'No,' yelled Alistair, 'that's one of Mum's dinner knives. She'll kill us.'

Colin knelt at the back door. He looked closely at the lock. No signs of rust. In fact the whole thing looked pretty new. Must have been a recent purchase from the Biggest Do-It-Yourself Hardware Centre In Greater London.

He put the blade of the knife into the groove in one of the screws and started turning.

'You can't do that,' yelled Alistair.

Colin could and he did.

The hospital looked exactly like Colin had hoped it would. It was big, almost as big as Buckingham Palace, and built out of great stone blocks.

Colin looked up at it, standing massive and calm while all around it the roaring London traffic tried to choke it with carbon monoxide and above it the pigeons bombarded it with ribbons of poo.

It didn't look worried at all.

Few exhaust fumes and a bit of pigeon poo doesn't worry me, it seemed to be saying. I've got the best doctor in the world in here.

Colin felt a weight being lifted off him.

He walked towards the main entrance, through a

car-park filled with the newest and shiniest Jags he'd ever seen.

Inside it was even better.

The ceiling was at least twice as high as the hospital in Sydney, and on the corridor walls were real oil paintings of important-looking men with beards and stethoscopes.

Famous doctors, thought Colin. The geniuses who gave us Modern Medicine and all its wondrous technology. The operating theatre and the X-ray machine and the Band-aid that doesn't leave a sticky black outline when you pull it off.

He moved down the corridor, peeking into rooms. Most of them had big dark wooden desks in them and ancient leather armchairs. Others were full of gleaming, modern equipment.

Colin was impressed. You didn't often come across blokes with those sorts of desks and those sorts of armchairs who knew how to operate that sort of equipment.

'You lost?'

Colin spun round. Looking at him was a nurse, her eyebrows raised.

'No, I'm right thanks,' said Colin.

She nodded and gave him a kind smile.

'Looked as though you were lost.'

'I was just checking that this is the best cancer hospital in London,' said Colin.

The nurse grinned and leant towards him.

'Best in London?' she said. 'It's the best in the world. People come in here, their relatives have already started squabbling over their furniture. When they leave, some of them, they go round to their Aunty Maud's, get their sideboard back and carry it home by themselves.'

She grinned again and walked off.

Colin grinned too. He had a vision of Luke, cured and laughing, staggering home from Bayliss's Department Store carrying the bunk bed with the built-in cubby house that had been number two on his Chrissie list.

Colin hurried along the corridor. At the end he turned left and found himself in a huge ward full of bustling nurses and rows of beds with patients in them.

Then he saw him, standing next to a bed, surrounded by student doctors.

The Best Doctor In The World.

He looked exactly like Colin had imagined he would. Tall and broad-shouldered, with a wise, important face and thick grey hair just like the Dad in Dynasty.

'Accessibility is paramount,' he said to the student doctors.

Colin's chest thumped with excitement.

He even spoke important.

'In other words,' said the doctor, 'the patient must always feel that he can speak to you, that you've got time for him.'

The student doctors scribbled furiously on their notepads, then went back to staring at the doctor in awe.

The doctor picked up the hand of the patient in the bed, patted it, put it back down and moved on to the next bed.

Now's my chance, thought Colin, blood pounding in his ears.

He pushed through the student doctors, got a stethoscope hooked round his arm, pulled himself free, and found himself in front of the doctor.

The doctor stared down at him.

Words rushed around in Colin's head. He opened his mouth and let them out.

'I know you're real busy here and everything but you've got to come to Australia and fix up Luke. They reckon he's gunna die but I just reckon they're being slack and you can do it, I know you can.'

The doctor frowned.

'Who is this?' he boomed.

'Luke,' said Colin, 'my brother.'

The doctor pointed to Colin.

'I mean who is this boy?' he thundered.

The student doctors looked at each other in alarm. A couple looked at their notepads.

'We'll pay your fare,' said Colin, 'or if you've got a Lear jet we'll pay the petrol.'

A couple of the student doctors tittered. Several patients grinned.

'Matron,' roared the doctor, and turned and swept along to the next bed.

Colin tried to follow, but a large Matron hurried across and grabbed his arm.

He stamped on her foot, pulled himself free and went after the doctor.

'Please,' yelled Colin, 'you've got to do it, it'll only take a few days, you've got to.'

The doctor turned and glared at the nurses who were standing all around, frozen.

'I am trying to do my rounds,' he roared, his face flushing red with anger. 'Will somebody please remove this child.'

Colin felt panic stabbing him in the guts.

It wasn't working.

The Best Doctor In The World hadn't put his hand on his shoulder and smiled down and said, 'Leave it to me, son.'

'He's got cancer,' pleaded Colin. 'He could die.'

'Everyone here has got cancer,' thundered the doctor, sweeping his arm around the ward. 'They could all die.'

Suddenly none of the patients were grinning.

'If your brother needs treatment, there are proper channels. I will not have my ward round disrupted like this.'

'Please,' said Colin.

The Worst Doctor In The World thumped his hand onto Colin's shoulder and glared down and roared, 'Go away!'

'No!' screamed Colin, throwing himself at the doctor. But before he could land a punch he was grabbed from behind by several pairs of hands and suddenly he was upside down and the doctor, also upside down, was getting smaller and smaller and then was gone.

Colin saw the corridor walls blurring past him. He kicked and struggled, but the two male nurses and the uniformed attendant had him in a bone-crusher grip.

They took him into an office and held him down in a chair while a supervisor gave him some forms that the patient's parent or guardian could fill out if the patient's doctor and/or senior medical administrator agreed.

Then the uniformed attendant marched Colin out of the hospital.

Chapter Ten

Colin sat on the kerb and felt a hot pricking in his eyes that meant either Arnie Strachan had just blown cigarette smoke in his face or he was going to cry.

Arnie Strachan was twelve thousand miles away, so it must be that he was going to cry.

Colin decided he wasn't going to cry.

He closed his eyes and thought of Dad. Dad never cried, not even the time Colin bowled a Malcolm Marshall special off an extra long run-up and it bounced crooked off a cow-pat and slammed Dad in the privates.

It's not a disaster, thought Colin.

He'd gone for the wrong doctor, that's all. He'd gone for the doctor who looked like The World's Best Doctor. He'd been fooled by a Dynasty haircut. The real World's Best Doctor was probably bald with glasses.

All Colin had to do was go back into the Best Cancer Hospital In London (avoiding the uniformed attendant) and find him.

He was wondering how best to avoid the uniformed attendant (should he smuggle himself in with the clean sheets or go in through the drains?) when he noticed something across the street.

A bloke sitting on the kerb.

Crying.

Not sniffing and blinking back prickles in his eyes, but really crying, his whole body shaking with massive sobs.

Colin realised he'd never seen a bloke really blub. Kids, yes, but not an adult bloke. Adults put on brave faces and said, 'Mmmm, I'm starving.'

Colin wondered why this one wasn't.

He went over.

'You OK?' he asked.

The bloke looked up at him, startled.

'No, I'm not, I'm crying,' he said and looked away and sniffed and blinked a few times. When he looked back up at Colin he'd stopped crying. 'But ta for asking,' he said and grinned.

He was much younger than Dad. He looked to Colin about the same age as Mr Blair at school, 25, except that Mr Blair didn't wear a leather jacket and didn't grin.

The bloke sniffed and wiped his eyes.

'I needed that,' he said.

Colin had only ever heard a bloke say that after a beer.

'Why did you need it?' he asked.

'I've got a friend in there who's very sick,' said the bloke, pointing to the hospital across the road. 'Normally I'm OK, but once a week I treat myself to a bit of a cry.'

Colin could tell from the way he swallowed after saying 'very sick' that the friend wasn't just a workmate or someone he played pool with.

Must be his girlfriend.

'Cancer?' asked Colin. He felt like booting himself in the bum. Course it was cancer.

The bloke opened his mouth to say something, then closed it and nodded. He looked closely at Colin.

'You're the one who was making all the commotion in the ward, right?'

'Colin Mudford,' said Colin, holding out his hand.

'Ted Caldicot,' replied the bloke, shaking it. 'What were you doing, pinching grapes?'

'No,' said Colin, 'trying to find a doctor for my brother.'

Ted looked down at the road and his soft voice, with its accent Colin couldn't quite place, became even softer.

'I'm sorry. Has your brother got cancer?'

At last. An adult who wasn't a doctor had actually said the word.

Colin sat down on the kerb next to Ted and told him about Luke and the Queen and the Best Doctor In The World.

By the time he'd finished, Ted was grinning again.

'Incredible,' he said. 'You, Colin, are an inspiration to us all. Come and have a cup of tea.'

The hospital cafeteria was full of people who looked exactly like they'd just been visiting other people with cancer. Long faces, round shoulders, bowed heads.

That was the first thing Colin noticed as he stood in the queue with Ted.

The second was Ted's tattoo.

It was a small one on the back of his hand. Leaves and flowers around a word Colin couldn't read properly. A foreign word.

'What does that say?' asked Colin, pointing to it.

'It's Welsh,' said Ted. 'Means "Forever".'

Colin was impressed. The only other tattoo he'd seen up close was Doug Beale's uncle's and that had said 'Death Before Disco'. 'Forever' was much better.

'Where I come from in Wales,' said Ted, 'people get them done when they're in love.'

'Has your friend got one?' asked Colin.

Ted nodded and turned away.

Colin felt like booting himself in the bum again.

But Ted had only turned away because they were at the front of the queue and a brawny woman in a white apron was waiting to serve them.

'Two teas love, ta,' said Ted, 'and thirty chocolate frogs.'

Thirty?

Colin thought he'd heard wrong, but there was the woman, grumpily counting out thirty of the little chocolate frogs in silver paper that you were supposed to buy while you waited for your change.

There were thirty-four in the box and Ted took the lot.

They found an empty table and put their teas on it.

Then Ted handed the box of frogs to Colin and climbed on to the table himself.

'Excuse me, ladies and gentlemen,' he said, 'excuse me.'

The low murmur of conversation in the room went even lower. People stared up at Ted.

Colin stared up at Ted. That's all he needed. A cup of tea with a loony.

'We're all here for the same reason,' said Ted to the frowning and suspicious faces looking up at him, 'and we've all got people in there who need us very much. What they don't need is for us to turn into misery-guts. If anyone here thinks they might be turning into a misery-guts, I'd strongly recommend a chocolate frog from my young friend.'

Colin felt the blood rush to his cheeks as all eyes turned to him.

For a moment there was nothing but a sea of frowning and suspicious faces.

Then a face just to his left broke into a smile and a hand reached into the box and took a frog. Another smile. Another hand. A murmur went round the room and smiles were breaking out all over the place.

'Go on, Col,' said Ted, jumping down, 'do the rounds.'

Colin took the box around the cafeteria and in two minutes there wasn't a frog left.

'Have to get some more of those in,' said the woman behind the counter, grinning hugely at Colin.

Colin didn't know what to say. He hadn't enjoyed himself so much for months.

He and Ted sat down and drank their tea.

'I've been thinking,' said Ted. 'I know a couple of the doctors here pretty well. What if I have a word to them about Luke?'

A jab of excitement hit Colin in the guts.

'Yes,' he said, 'please.'

'OK,' said Ted. 'Tomorrow's Saturday. I don't know if they're rostered on for the weekend. Why don't you meet me here at midday on Monday and we'll go and see them then.'

'Thanks,' said Colin, 'thanks a lot.'

'I've got to go back to my friend now,' said Ted. 'Write the name of Luke's hospital down for me.'

Colin was so excited he could hardly hold the pen.

He went back to the house, replaced the back door lock, calmed Alistair down, and by the time Aunty Iris and Uncle Bob got home, he was sitting in an armchair looking as though he'd just had a quiet day with the Do-It-Yourself magazines instead of swinging punches at pathologists, meeting incredible blokes who blubbed and gave away chocolate frogs, and arranging to see doctors who were going to save Luke's life.

After tea Mum and Dad rang.

'I haven't said anything about the Buckingham Palace business,' said Aunty Iris as she handed the phone to Colin, 'and if you carry on behaving yourself I hope I won't have to.'

Mum asked Colin how he was and he said fine. He asked how Luke was and she said that Luke was as well as could be expected. She said she and Dad were as well as could be expected too.

Colin could hardly hear her because she wasn't using her usual long-distance voice. Her voice sounded small and very weary and very sad.

He glanced round to make sure Aunty Iris had gone back into the living-room.

'Mum,' he said, 'everything's going to be OK. You don't have to worry any more. I'm going to see one of London's top cancer doctors on Monday and he's going to cure Luke.'

He waited for her relief and delight to come pouring out of the phone. But all he heard were faint sobs coming from the other end.

'Mum,' he said, 'are you all right?'

Then he remembered that mums sometimes cried when they were very happy.

Aunty Iris and Uncle Bob announced next morning that they were going to take Colin out over the weekend to get his mind off 'things'.

Saturday morning they spent at The Biggest Do-It-Yourself Hardware Centre in Greater London.

Colin bought a small screwdriver.

'Never know when you're going to need one,' he said, and Uncle Bob nodded approvingly.

'Alistair, stop biting your nails,' said Aunty Iris.

In the afternoon they went to the local park.

Colin tried to teach Alistair spin bowling, but it wasn't easy because it was snowing lightly and the ball wouldn't turn off the pitch. And every time

Alistair bent over to bat, Aunty Iris would call out, 'Alistair, don't hunch your shoulders.'

Then she noticed that next to the park was a large cemetery. Colin saw her look at the graves, glance anxiously at him, and before he could send down another outswinging leg-break they were all back in the car.

Colin wanted to tell her that it didn't matter if he saw graves because Luke wasn't going to die, but he decided not to. He didn't want to risk them chucking a mental over the back door lock and replacing it with an electronic alarm system or something. Not till after he'd seen Ted's friend on Monday.

On Sunday they went to an Air Show.

Formations of fighter planes belching coloured smoke swooped low over the crowd and deafened everyone.

'Luke'd enjoy this,' Colin yelled to Aunty Iris.

He saw her face fall.

'Almost as much as I am,' he added hastily.

She gave a relieved smile.

Later, when he bought a plastic model of a Harrier Jump Jet, he didn't tell her it was for Luke. But he glowed inside at the thought of arriving in Sydney with Ted's friend and the one model plane Luke had never been able to find in Australia.

As they were leaving the Air Show, they saw an air-force officer with gold braid on his cap strolling around chatting to the public.

'Big nob in the Queen's Squadron,' said Uncle Bob. 'Bloody show-off. He should be flying people to Spain for their holidays, not poncing about with pink smoke coming out of his rear end.'

While Aunty Iris told Uncle Bob to mind his language, Colin ran over to the officer.

'S'cuse me,' he said, 'next time you see the Queen could you tell her it doesn't matter about Colin Mudford's letter now cause I've met a bloke who knows a doctor?'

The officer looked at him blankly. Colin wondered if fighter pilots ever got brain damage from the G-forces.

'Luke, my brother,' he explained, 'he's going to be OK.'

'Oh,' said the officer, brightening. 'Right-oh. Jolly good. I'll tell her.'

Chapter Eleven

First thing Monday, as soon as Aunty Iris and Uncle Bob had locked the doors and gone, Colin rang Qantas.

'Which days this week have you got empty seats going to Australia,' he asked, 'and before you say anything, it's not a school project.'

The man at Qantas said there were seats available on every flight.

'They can't be near the dunnies,' said Colin, 'one of the passengers is a very eminent doctor.'

The man at Qantas said seat allocation took place at the airport, but eminent doctors were rarely sat near the toilets.

'He'll probably be travelling incognito,' said Colin, 'so other passengers don't bother him with their varicose veins and sore fingers.'

In the kitchen, Alistair was standing in front of the back door lock.

'I can't let you do it,' he said. 'You fluked it on Friday. If you take that lock off again today Mum and Dad'll catch you.'

Colin got out his screwdriver.

'We'll be eating cold baked beans for a week,' pleaded Alistair.

'I like cold baked beans,' said Colin, advancing towards the back door.

Alistair lunged at him and grabbed the screwdriver. Colin kept hold of it and they struggled, Colin grabbing Alistair's arm, Alistair putting his other arm round Colin's neck and trying to pull him over backwards.

'I don't want to hurt you,' panted Alistair, hurting Colin, 'just give me the screwdriver.'

Because Alistair was bigger and stronger, Colin gave him the screwdriver.

Then he told him about The Best Cancer Hospital In London and Ted and how Ted's doctor friend was going to save Luke.

Alistair handed Colin back the screwdriver.

'Wait till you get back to Australia,' he said wistfully as Colin started to unscrew the lock, 'you're going to be a blinking hero.'

Colin ran into the hospital cafeteria at exactly midday. He looked around for Ted. There he was, sitting at a table in the corner with a cup of tea.

Colin hurried over.

Then stopped.

There was something about the way Ted was sitting, shoulders slumped, staring at the tea. Colin realised what it was. Ted looked exactly like the people had on Friday before they'd got their chocolate frogs.

Ted hadn't seen him yet so he ducked over to the counter and made a quick purchase.

'Only one?' said the brawny woman in the white apron. 'That won't go far.'

Colin moved stealthily over to where Ted sat, still staring at the tea. He quickly sat down opposite and put the chocolate frog on the table in front of Ted.

Ted looked at it, startled, then his face relaxed. He looked up at Colin.

'Hi, digger,' he said.

He'd cheered up, but not a lot.

Colin decided not to ask him about his sick friend. He didn't look as though he wanted to talk about it right now.

'This doctor friend of yours,' said Colin, 'is he a quick packer?'

'A quick what?'

'A quick packer. Does he do his packing quickly when he's going somewhere? Or is he like Russell Hinch's mum, always making lists and losing them?'

'Colin . . .' said Ted, taking a deep breath.

'Doesn't matter,' said Colin, 'he doesn't have to bring much.'

'Colin . . .' said Ted.

'He can borrow some of Dad's shirts. Unless he's got a really fat neck.'

'Colin,' said Ted, standing up, 'I think we'd better go and see him.'

'Oh,' said Colin, 'he has got a really fat neck.'

* * *

'Colin,' said Ted, 'this is Doctor Graham.'

'Hello, Colin,' said Dr Graham, holding out his hand.

Colin shook it, looking at Dr Graham's neck. It wasn't fat at all, what was Ted on about?

Dr Graham was tall and slim and, Colin was interested to note, balding with glasses.

'Doctor Graham is one of the most experienced cancer experts in the world,' said Ted.

'Great,' said Colin. 'When can you leave? They've got seats on all flights, including tonight. What's your collar size, by the way?'

'Have a seat, Colin,' said Dr Graham.

Colin sat on a hard leather chair.

Dr Graham sat on the corner of his big, polished-wood desk.

'You don't have to worry about getting a seat near the dunnies,' said Colin. 'I've checked it out. You're OK cause you're eminent.'

'Colin,' said Dr Graham, 'I've been in touch with the hospital in Sydney where Luke is.'

Colin was impressed. They didn't mess around, these top blokes.

'I rang early this morning and I spoke to one of the doctors treating Luke,' continued Dr Graham.

'Mum and Dad'll want to pay you back for that call,' said Colin. 'Or perhaps Dad'll just give you a couple of shirts.'

Dr Graham shifted forward slightly on the corner of his desk.

'The doctor told me exactly what type of cancer

Luke has, Colin. He told me the exact locations and exactly how far advanced it is. His diagnosis is correct, Colin. Luke can't be cured. He's going to die.'

Colin stared.

His body had stopped working.

His mind had stopped working.

He was dimly aware of Ted touching his shoulder and someone else standing close to him. A nurse.

'Bull!' Colin heard himself say.

The doctor was still talking.

'. . . greatly increased recovery rate these days for young people with cancer. Up around fifty per cent. I'm afraid Luke is one of the unlucky ones and there's nothing I or anyone can do.'

'Bull!' Colin heard himself shout.

His body still wouldn't work.

He watched the doctor open a large book and hold it up so Colin could see a diagram of a person with coloured wires running all through their body.

'Glandular system,' Colin heard the doctor say, and 'very rare type of cancer' and a whole lot of technical stuff.

'Colin,' said the nurse, 'would you like a pill to make you feel better?'

No he wouldn't. He felt angry and that was exactly how he wanted to feel.

Suddenly his body started working.

He stood up, pushed the nurse aside and ran for the door, through the door, down the corridor, nurses and patients looming up and bouncing off him, down another corridor, Ted's shouts behind him, past the uniformed attendant, out into the cold bright air, cars parked everywhere, bumping into bumper bars and icy paintwork, to a corner, down into a corner, brick walls all around him, where hot tears of anger poured down his face and he didn't care.

Sssssssssssssssssss.

The search party had given up.

The doctors and the nurses and the uniformed attendant and Ted had hunted through the car-park and the hospital grounds and then gone back inside.

Why did they want to find him, thought Colin bitterly. To make excuses about why the doctors couldn't stop Luke dying?

Sssssssssssssssssss.

He knew why. They were failures.

Sssssssssssssssssss.

Failures.

Sssssssssssssssssss.

Colin watched as the air hissed out of the tyre of the Mercedes. Soon the tyre was flat, like the other three on the car.

Colin crawled along to the next one, a Jag.

Sssssssssssssssssss.

How dare they drive cars with automatic aerials and dual anti-lock braking systems and wipers on the headlamps when they couldn't even cure cancer?

Sssssssssssssssssss.

How dare people use up all the technology on cars

like this, and jumbo jets, and microwave ovens, and spray-on stain removers that worked like magic, when they couldn't even stop Luke dying?

Sssssssssssssssssss.

Failures.

Sssssssssssssssssss.

Colin looked back along the row of Jags and Mercedes and BMWs and Audis, all with flat tyres.

Serve them right.

He crawled along to the next car.

Leaning against it was Ted. He pulled Colin to his feet.

'You'd better scarper,' he said. 'I'll look after this lot.' He pushed a piece of paper into Colin's pocket. 'Leg it.'

Colin looked away.

He stared at the last deflating tyre on the Jag.

Sssssssssssssssssss.

Failure.

It was saying it to him.

He ran.

Chapter Twelve

He'd failed.

The thought made him ache all over as he put the lock back on the door.

Angry tears filled his eyes again and he couldn't see the screw or the screwdriver.

Why am I bothering with this, he thought. I couldn't care less if they catch me or not. They can lock me in a cupboard between 8.30 and 5.30 each day for all I care. I deserve it.

He let the screw and the screwdriver fall to the floor and stood up.

Alistair grabbed them and started screwing the lock on frantically.

'They'll be back in ten minutes,' he shouted.

Colin went upstairs and threw himself on his bed.

He'd failed.

He pictured Mum and Dad meeting his plane in Sydney, their weary faces lit up with hope and pride, waiting to catch sight of him walking towards them with the doctor who could save Luke.

Then seeing him, alone.

Their disappointment.

Colin buried his face in the pillow. He could never go back.

Later he heard whispering outside his room.

'He's just sort of lying there.'

'Asleep?'

'Think so.'

'It's delayed shock, I saw it on TV once, sometimes it can take weeks to crop up. Alistair, leave your scalp alone.'

'Had to happen sooner or later, poor kid. Alistair, you heard what your mother said.'

'Wonder if we should get the doctor in?'

'No, plenty of rest's what he needs, I'd say.'

'I'm just worried he might be sickening for something.'

'Let him rest.'

Don't worry, Aunty Iris, thought Colin. I'm not going to get sick. Not now I've decided what to do.

Later still, as he lay in the darkness staring upwards, mind racing, he became aware of someone standing next to the bed.

'Colin,' said Alistair, 'are you awake?'

Colin said he was.

'I got the lock on in time,' said Alistair.

'Thanks,' said Colin. 'Sorry about that.'

'And I didn't tell them about your friend's doctor friend.'

'Thanks.'

'Didn't it work out?'

Colin told him.

'Oh,' said Alistair.

'But it's OK,' said Colin, 'because I'm going to university to discover a cure for cancer.'

'Oh,' said Alistair. 'Brilliant.'

Colin switched on the bedside lamp.

He saw Alistair thinking about something and looking uncomfortable.

'By the time you get to university,' said Alistair, 'won't it be a bit, you know, for Luke. Late.'

'No,' said Colin. 'I'm going tomorrow.

'Tomorrow? But you're too young. And you've got to pass exams before you can go to university.'

'I haven't got time for all that,' said Colin, 'so I'm starting tomorrow.'

'They won't let you in.'

'We'll see.'

'If you change your mind,' said Alistair, 'I've got a new board game. Explorers. We could play it tomorrow.'

'I won't change my mind,' said Colin.

Next morning Colin had changed his mind.

'The Amazon?' said Alistair, wide-eyed.

'It's a river,' said Colin, 'in South America.'

'I know,' said Alistair. 'It's miles away.'

Colin propped himself up in bed and opened the atlas. Aunty Iris had insisted he stay in bed all day and Colin, figuring bed was as good a place as any to plan a trip to South America, had agreed.

He ran his finger along the River Amazon.

'There are ancient tribes that have lived there undisturbed for centuries,' he said. 'I saw them on TV. They make all their own medicine. I reckon in all that time, without being distracted by having to invent jumbo jets and microwave ovens and BMWs, they'd have discovered a cure for cancer.'

Alistair looked doubtful.

'Ancient tribes know heaps of things we don't,' said Colin. 'I met an Aboriginal bloke in the supermarket once who knew how to cure indigestion with bits of a lizard.'

'And you're going to go to the Amazon and find an ancient tribe and get them to tell you their cure for cancer?' said Alistair.

'Yes,' said Colin. 'I'm leaving tomorrow.'

'What if they haven't discovered one?'

'I'll go to Africa, they've got heaps of ancient tribes there.'

Alistair stared at him.

'Do you know how much it costs to fly to South America and Africa?' he demanded.

'I've got my air ticket back to Australia,' said Colin, 'I can have stopovers wherever I like.'

'Not if the airline doesn't fly there,' said Alistair.

'All right,' said Colin, 'I'll stow away on a cargo ship.'

Alistair stared at Colin again, then walked out of the room shaking his head.

Colin lay back and stared at the ceiling. He saw himself stepping off a cargo ship in Sydney and handing Mum and Dad the cancer cure in a small, jewelled bottle, and he saw the look in their eyes of relief and admiration.

Alistair came back into the room.

Here we go, thought Colin, what problem has he thought of this time?

'Colin?'

'Yes?'

'Can I come with you?'

It wasn't until that afternoon, when Colin was going through his pockets looking for his air ticket so he could ring Quantas and find out if he could have a stopover in South America, that he found the piece of paper.

He looked at it, puzzled for a moment.

Then he remembered Ted pushing it into his pocket in the hospital car-park.

And he remembered he'd left Ted with all the flat tyres. What if Ted had got into trouble for that?

Been arrested?

Colin looked at the piece of paper again.

It was Ted's address.

He should really go and see if Ted was all right, specially after what Ted had done for him.

Can't go now, he thought, Aunty Iris and Uncle Bob'll be back in an hour.

I'll go tomorrow.

After all, it would only mean putting off South America for one day.

Chapter Thirteen

It was a grimy street with tough-looking kids hanging around on the corner, and an old car without wheels or seats parked outside a laundromat.

Colin found Ted's place, an old house divided up into flats. He checked Ted's flat number against the list of numbers and names written up in marker pen on the wall next to the front door.

Then he noticed, further along the wall, a word spray-painted on the bricks in big red letters. The last couple of letters were stretched, as if whoever had done it had started running before they'd finished.

QUEENS.

Funny, thought Colin, surely she wouldn't own a run-down old place like this.

The front door was open, and Colin had to climb right to the top floor to find Ted's flat.

He knocked on the door, hoping fervently Ted was in. He didn't fancy hanging about waiting. Those kids on the corner had looked like trouble with knobs on.

Ted's voice came from inside the flat.

'Who is it?'

'Colin,' called Colin. 'Mudford.'

'Hang on.'

There was a silence, then Colin heard grunting and a table leg squeaking on lino. The grunting got louder, and there was the sound of something being dragged across the floor.

The door opened.

Ted stood there, leaning against the door frame, panting and wincing with pain. He looked at Colin and forced his face into a grin.

'Well,' he said, 'what a surprise. Come in.'

Colin stared.

On one side of Ted's face was a huge bruise and one of his feet was wrapped in bandages.

'Give over,' said Ted, 'you've seen minor injuries before. Here, give us your shoulder.'

Ted pushed the door shut and, using Colin for support, hobbled across the room, dragging his bandaged foot across the floor. He flopped down on to a bed in the corner.

'What happened to you?' asked Colin.

An awful thought occurred to him.

Perhaps Ted had been bashed up at the hospital by irate Jag and Mercedes and BMW owners.

'Local junior hoods,' said Ted, 'jumped me last night as I was coming back from the hospital. Belted me round the head with a piece of wood and jumped up and down on me for a few minutes. Cut my foot.'

'Why?' asked Colin, horrified.

'Don't think they like me,' answered Ted with a grin.

'What about the police?' said Colin.

'They don't like me much either,' said Ted, still grinning. 'Anyway, it was dark, there was a whole crowd of them, I had my eyes closed most of the time. Not much point going to the police.'

Then Colin froze.

On the floor at his feet was a huge red puddle.

'It's OK,' said Ted, laughing, 'it's not blood. It's tomato soup. I was trying to get myself some food and my foot gave way.'

'I'll clean it up,' said Colin.

'Thanks,' said Ted, 'but actually there's something more urgent you can help me with. I'm due at the hospital in an hour. Not a chance of making it in this state but Griff's going to be worried when I don't turn up. I can't even get down the stairs to ring up. Could you go and ring for me?'

'No problem,' said Colin. 'But first I'm going to get you something to eat.'

'Delicious,' said Ted, taking another mouthful. 'Best curry I've had in ages. Really like the glacé cherries.'

'Needs a bit of salt,' said Colin. 'I couldn't find any in the kitchen.'

'Over there,' said Ted.

The salt shaker was on a small coffee table. Next to it, Colin saw, in a carved wood frame, was a photo of a man about Ted's age. In the corner of the photo was written 'To Ted, Forever, Griff.'

'Griff's always moaning at me for never putting things away,' said Ted. His voice went quieter. 'Six years we've been together and as soon as he goes into hospital I'm back to my old untidy habits.'

Colin stared at the photo.

Forever.

He knew that men sometimes fell in love with each other and that it was called being gay. The idea had never worried him that much, though he didn't think he ever would himself.

Then he remembered the graffiti on the wall downstairs.

Queens.

He'd heard men at barbeques say queens when they were talking about gay men. They usually sneered as they said it.

He looked at Ted, and saw that Ted was watching him carefully.

'Is that why they bashed you up,' said Colin, 'cause you and Griff are in love?'

Ted's face relaxed and he nodded.

Pathetic, thought Colin. All the blokes in the world doing really mean and cruel stuff and getting away without even a smack round the ear and here's a bloke getting totally bashed up for being in love with another bloke.

'Colin,' said Ted, 'would you be able to give the hospital a ring now?'

'Would you like me to go and visit Griff for you?' said Colin. He hadn't planned that, it had just popped out.

'That's very good of you, Colin,' said Ted.

Colin looked at him. Ted hadn't said it in the way

that meant 'yes please', he'd said it in the way that meant 'I don't think you should.'

Ted took a deep breath.

'Colin, Griff hasn't just got cancer. He's got cancer because he's also got a virus called AIDS.'

Colin had heard of that. The government had sent a booklet around about it. He knew it was a virus a lot of people were very scared of. He also knew you couldn't catch it visiting people in hospital.

'I don't mind,' he said.

For a moment Colin thought he was in the wrong room.

Ted had drawn a map showing him how to get to Griff's ward, but either they'd moved the ward or Ted wasn't very good at maps.

Colin hadn't dared ask any of the doctors or nurses for directions in case they'd recognized him as The Phantom Tyre Deflator. OK, Ted had said that following the description he'd given the uniformed attendant after Colin had legged it, hospital security were looking for a middle-aged tow-truck driver with a red beard and a limp, but you couldn't be too careful.

Wandering through the maze of corridors, Colin had suddenly seen a ward with the number Ted had marked on the map, and had gone in.

Now he was looking at the thinnest man he'd ever seen.

This couldn't be Griff.

In the photo Griff had bulging arms and his smiling mouth made his face sort of bunch out at the cheeks.

The man lying with his eyes closed in the bed in front of Colin had arms like cricket stumps and his cheeks were so thin they were almost hollow.

Colin looked at the chart on the end of the bed.

G. Price.

The name was right, but perhaps there was more than one G. Price in the hospital. Perhaps this one was Garry or Greg or Gavin. A jockey who'd gone on a diet and overdone it.

The man opened his eyes and looked at Colin.

'Hello,' he said.

'G'day,' said Colin. 'Are you Griff?'

The man nodded.

'I'm Colin,' said Colin. 'I'm here cause Ted's a bit crook today. It's OK but, it's nothing serious. Here, he wrote you a note.'

Colin handed Griff the note and watched while he read it.

AIDS must be a pretty awful virus, he thought, to give you rings under your eyes like that.

'You're sure it's not serious?' asked Griff.

'No, it's just that he can't walk on his foot. Doctor says he'll be right in a few days.'

'He didn't say how many days?'

'Don't think so,' said Colin.

Griff sighed and seemed to sink even further into the bedclothes.

'Well, it's very kind of you to come, Colin,' he said.

'Here,' said Colin, 'Ted gave me some stuff for you.'

He rummaged in the supermarket bag he'd brought with him and took out a library book, some toothpaste, and some tangerines.

Griff struggled up onto his elbows to look and he broke into a grin when he saw the tangerines.

'You're an angel,' he said, and started to peel one.

Colin put a pillow behind Griff's back to prop him up.

'I always thought that when I saw my first angel it'd have wings and a halo,' said Griff, 'not freckles and elastic-sided boots. Want some?'

He held out half a tangerine.

'Or would you rather peel your own?'

Colin knew why Griff was giving him the choice. Some people were scared a person with AIDS could give it to you real easy, like a cold or nits. Ted had explained that you could only catch it off stuff from inside the body, blood and stuff like that.

'Thanks,' said Colin. He took the half tangerine.

They talked for ages.

Griff told how he and Ted had met eight years before while they were both working in a sheet metal factory in Wales. Then, last year, the factory had closed down and they'd spent months trying to get other jobs.

Unemployment in Wales was so bad they hadn't been able to. So they'd come to London to look for work. A week after they arrived, Griff had got sick and was told he had AIDS.

Colin told Griff about Australia, in particular Doug Beale's trail bike and the time he drove into Arnie Strachan's chook pen. Arnie had been so mad he went round to Doug's place with a pair of sheep shearing clippers and clipped Doug's Mum's shag-pile carpet.

Griff laughed so much Colin was worried he'd hurt himself.

'What are you doing over here?' asked Griff.

Colin wondered whether to tell him about Luke.

He decided not to. It'd only depress him.

Colin was trying not to think about it himself.

Chapter Fourteen

'But I'm all packed,' said Alistair. 'I thought we were leaving today. I've taken the lock off and everything.'

'Something's come up,' said Colin. 'It'll only be a couple more days.'

'A couple more days? I've made sandwiches. They'll go stale.'

Colin saw that looped across Alistair's chest was the Buckingham Palace wall rope. The several bent wire coat hangers tied to the end of it clattered against the ironing cupboard as Alistair sat down sulkily on the kitchen stool.

'Took me ages to make this grappling-iron to get us onto the cargo ship,' said Alistair. 'I'll have to pull it to bits if we're not going today. Dad goes spare if there's nothing to hang his shirt on.'

'Hide it under your bed,' said Colin. 'I'll buy some more hangers while I'm out.'

'Where are you going, anyway, that's so important?' sulked Alistair.

'Just helping a mate out,' said Colin.

'That's all very well,' said Alistair, 'but while you're doing that, the ancient tribes of the Amazon are probably giving their cure for cancer to some Swiss chemical company who'll put it in pills and sell them for a million pounds each.'

Ted wasn't grinning today.

He was lying on the bed looking at his bandaged foot as if he wished he could chop it off.

'Perishing thing,' he muttered. 'Doctor says it'll be another week before I can walk on it.'

Colin looked at him sadly.

A whole week without seeing the bloke you were in love with was pretty tough.

'OK,' he said, trying to take Ted's mind off it, 'that's fruit, shampoo and cough lollies.' He put them all into the plastic bag. 'Anything else?'

'You don't have to do this, you know,' said Ted, looking at him. 'You've got problems of your own.'

'Does Griff like curry?' asked Colin. 'I could take him in some curry.'

It was on his third visit to Griff that Colin had the idea.

A nurse wheeled a patient past the doorway of Griff's ward and the idea hit Colin like a lunch box from a low-flying cropduster.

Of course, why hadn't he thought of it before?

He finished telling Griff about Des Phipp's elder brother who could fit a whole meat pie into his mouth and still have room for the sauce, and then it was time for Griff's shower.

Colin said goodbye and went out into the main

corridor. He went up to the busiest nurse he could see, one who was hurrying along with an armful of bedpans and was about to drop them.

'Excuse me,' said Colin, 'where do they keep the wheelchairs?'

'Ugh ugh ugh,' said the nurse, who had a clipboard in her mouth. She didn't stop, but flipped her head towards a side corridor.

There was only one door at the end of it.

Colin held his breath as he opened it. Inside were ten or more neatly-folded wheelchairs.

As he walked out of the hospital wheeling one of them, he kept telling himself not to run, not to bow his head, not to look guilty.

After all, if a hospital had wheelchairs for its patients, why shouldn't it have them for its visitors too?

After a wobbly start, the wheelchair was a huge success.

Getting Ted down the stairs was the problem at first, until Colin went and asked the Polish man in the bottom flat if he could help.

It turned out the Polish man had a brother in Australia and he and his wife helped Colin carry Ted all the way down the stairs and into the street.

'You're a genius,' shouted Ted as Colin wheeled him towards the tube station.

Colin considered asking Ted to put that in writing and send it to Mr Blair at school.

* * *

Ted and Griff were so pleased to see each other that Colin suddenly felt like an intruder.

Give them a bit of time alone, he thought.

He slipped out of the room, muttering that he had to go to the loo.

In fact, to kill time, he went for a wander through some of the other wards.

Room after room full of seriously ill people.

None of them with any reason to feel happy, thought Colin sadly as he walked on.

But each time he went into a new ward, something struck him afresh. Something so obvious it would have made him shrug and say 'so what' if he'd been told about it a month before.

Now, each time he saw it, he felt a strange pang inside.

The sick people who had their families and loved ones around their beds all looked happier than the ones who didn't.

When Colin got back to Griff's ward, Griff was sitting up and Ted was sitting next to him on the bed.

They both smiled when they saw Colin and beckoned him to them.

'We know you probably don't like soppy stuff,' said Ted, 'but we both just want to say thanks.'

Colin felt his insides go all warm and runny.

Who said he didn't like soppy stuff?

'You'll probably never know how important this

time is to us,' said Griff softly, 'or how precious a gift you've given us.'

'Now that,' said Ted grinning, 'was soppy.'

'Next Monday?' wailed Alistair. 'But I thought we were going today.'

'Ted'll be back on his feet then,' said Colin. 'Once he can visit Griff by himself we'll go.'

Alistair slumped onto the kitchen stool. The jungle first-aid kit slung around his neck clunked against the ironing cupboard. The lid came off and a couple of hundred kelp tablets rattled around on the floor.

'Mum and Dad are getting suspicious,' said Alistair. 'Mum walked into my room yesterday while I was practising sucking blood out of a snakebite and she thought I was kissing my hand. She said if she catches me doing it again I'll have to see a psychiatrist.'

'Well don't do it again,' said Colin. 'Practise on a cushion.'

'That's all very well,' said Alistair, 'but while I'm wasting time practising on a cushion the ancient tribes of South America are probably talking to an advertising agency about marketing their cure for cancer themselves.'

'That's if they've got one,' said Colin.

The next day Ted had to see his doctor for a check-up on his foot, so Colin wheeled him to the surgery.

The doctor was out on an emergency call and the receptionist told them he could be gone an hour or more. Ted and Colin agreed that Colin would go and spend a couple of hours with Griff, then come back and collect Ted and take him in.

Griff looked worse than Colin had ever seen him.

He was lying on his back, staring at the ceiling, making a faint rasping noise as he breathed. He didn't even smile when he saw Colin.

To cheer him up, Colin told him about the Bishop sisters who went swimming in their dad's water tank and Bronwyn Bishop lost a contact lens so they let all the water out to look for it.

Griff didn't even smile at that.

Oh well, thought Colin, you've probably got to understand how scarce water is out our way in December.

He started telling Griff about Wal Petersen's Holden Kingswood which had so much rust in it you could see the road through the floor.

He thought that was of pretty universal interest, specially with Wal Petersen being a policeman, but half-way through Griff put his hand on Colin's arm.

'I don't really feel like talking today,' he said.

Colin felt awful. Poor bloke's feeling real crook and I'm rabbiting on about police corruption.

'That's OK,' said Colin, 'no sweat. I'll go, eh?'

'No,' said Griff faintly, 'I like having someone here.'

So Colin sat quietly, watching Griff.

He wondered if it was possible to make someone

feel better by telepathy. Why not, he thought, people can bend spoons.

He tried it.

It seemed to work.

Every few minutes Griff looked over at him, and, seeing him there, seemed to relax.

Later that afternoon, when Colin returned with Ted, Griff looked much better.

Chapter Fifteen

'Tomorrow?' shrieked Alistair.

Colin nodded.

'You said today,' yelled Alistair. 'You said today would definitely be the day. You said Ted would be back on his feet today and that we would definitely be going to South America today.'

'I know,' said Colin quietly.

'I've been waiting for over a week,' shouted Alistair. 'I haven't been sleeping, I've got nerve rashes all over me, Mum says she's never seen my dandruff so bad.'

He rubbed his hair and a cloud of dandruff floated down onto his home-made grappling iron and his jungle first-aid kit.

'I'm sorry,' said Colin, 'but there's one more thing I've got to do.'

'What,' said Alistair bitterly, 'go and find another million people in hospital to visit?'

'The wheelchair,' said Colin. 'Ted's taking it back to the hospital this morning. What if he's caught with it and they ban him from the hospital? I took it out, it's me who should take it back.'

'If we don't go today,' said Alistair, 'I'm telling Mum and Dad about you taking the lock off every day and sneaking out. And then you'll never get to South America.'

Colin stared at Alistair's red, angry face. He saw Alistair meant it.

He felt desperation grip his chest.

'I've got to stop him trying to take it back,' he said. 'I've been thinking about it all weekend. If they ban him from the hospital he can't visit Griff.'

'And if I tell,' said Alistair, 'you can't visit the ancient tribes of the Amazon.'

Colin felt a very strong urge to belt Alistair round the head with the jungle first-aid kit.

Instead he thought fast.

'Ok,' he said, 'I'll be back here by two-thirty. We'll leave then.'

'You'd better be,' said Alistair.

Colin sprinted towards the hospital, the brown paper bag clutched tightly in one hand.

If I'm too late, he thought, I'll boot myself all over London.

He hadn't planned to stop at the fruit shop next to the tube station, but as he'd been hurrying past he'd seen them and the thought had hit him how much Griff would like them.

Australian mandarins.

Colin ran round the corner towards the main gates, brown paper bag flapping wildly, and saw Ted.

His first feeling was relief.

Ted wasn't grappling with the uniformed attendant and doctors weren't pulling the wheelchair from his grasp and policemen weren't running at him from every side.

His next feeling was concern. Ted was sitting on the kerb sobbing into his hands.

Colin stopped. He watched Ted's body shake and heave with the crying and wondered what he should do.

Then he remembered Ted's words the day Colin had first seen him, in much the same position, doing much the same thing.

'Once a week I treat myself to a bit of a cry,' he'd said.

Of course, thought Colin. Poor bloke, it's been nearly two weeks since then and this is probably the first one he's had.

He decided not to interrupt. Let him blub till he felt better, then they'd both go in and see Griff.

But where was the wheelchair?

Colin looked around, panic building inside him.

No wheelchair.

Was that why Ted was crying, because while he'd been buying mandarins Ted had been trying to sneak the wheelchair back in and had been caught and told never to set foot in the hospital again?

Colin ran over to him, boots thumping on the road.

Ted looked up and as soon as Colin saw Ted's eyes, even before Ted had managed to take a huge ragged breath and get the words out, Colin knew.

* * *

The numbness came to Colin immediately and was still there an hour later as he stood next to Ted in a small room in the hospital looking at Griff.

So still.

'He died this morning,' said Ted softly.

Colin looked at Griff lying still in the bed.

I'm not crying, he thought, why aren't I crying?

He heard himself speaking from a long way off.

'Were you here?'

'Yes I was,' said Ted. 'I've been here all night.'

Somewhere very distant from the numbness in his mind, Colin felt glad.

He remembered what Griff had said. 'You'll probably never know how important this time is to us.'

'His parents are coming this afternoon,' said Ted. 'They're taking him back to Wales for his funeral.'

Colin had never heard Griff mention his parents.

'Why didn't they come and visit him?' he asked.

'I don't know,' said Ted. 'I think it was too painful for them.'

What about Griff, thought Colin. How's a bloke meant to feel when he's crooker than a dog and his own family pikes out?

Poor bloke must have missed them.

Then, out of the blue, he found himself wondering if Luke was missing him.

He was late.

He sprinted from the tube station back to the house as fast as he could. Saying goodbye to Griff had taken a while, saying goodbye to Ted had taken even longer.

Colin ran harder to stop himself feeling sad.

He'd wanted to tell Ted about South America, but at the last minute he hadn't. He'd had a feeling Ted would tell him that if any ancient tribes in South America or Africa did have a cure for cancer, there'd have been a documentary about it on TV.

He ran down the side of the house and burst in through the back door.

The kitchen was empty.

'Alistair,' he yelled, 'I'm back.'

Aunty Iris stepped out of the dining-room.

Colin's guts went cold.

In her shaking hand was the back door lock.

'I'm very, very disappointed in you, Colin Mudford,' she said. 'We invited you over here to take your mind off things and all you've done is deceive us and lie to us.'

Colin tried to say 'sorry' but his mouth wouldn't work.

Aunty Iris's voice suddenly went very loud. 'South America, are you out of your mind? Do you know what the sun does to Alistair's skin?'

'Sorry,' said Colin.

'Bit late to apologize now,' said Aunty Iris, 'after you've been galavanting all over London with unsuitable types.'

'I haven't.'

'Don't try and deny it, my lad. I finally got the

names out of Alistair. Ted and Griff or whatever it is.'

'They weren't unsuitable,' said Colin.

'How do we know,' said Aunty Iris, waving the back door lock, 'since we've never had the pleasure of meeting them?'

Later that evening, Alistair crept into Colin's room.

'Sorry I blabbed,' he said, 'Mum told me keeping secrets would make my scalp worse.'

'Doesn't matter,' said Colin, staring at the wall. 'If the ancient tribes had a cure for cancer we'd have seen it on TV by now.'

'Yeah,' said Alistair, 'probably.'

There was a pause.

'Sorry I blabbed about Ted. You probably won't be able to see him any more now.'

'Yes I will,' said Colin.

'How come?' said Alistair.

Colin rolled over and faced Alistair.

'I've invited him to tea.'

'More tea Ted?' asked Aunty Iris.

'No thanks,' said Ted.

Silence descended once more onto the tea table.

This is a disaster, thought Colin.

He looked at Ted, sitting glumly at the end of the table. Was this the same bloke who'd lit up a roomful of gloomy faces with a handful of chocolate frogs?

He looked at Aunty Iris biting her lip and Uncle

Bob staring at the floor and Alistair staring at the ceiling.

He tried desperately to think of something to say.

It was no good, he wasn't in the mood for conversation either. He felt all tight and hollow inside, like he needed a good cry.

He'd been trying to cry half the night, thinking of Mum and Dad and their faces when they saw him get off the plane with no doctor and no little jewelled bottle.

No tears had come.

'What do you do for a crust, Ted?' asked Uncle Bob.

'I'm unemployed,' said Ted.

Silence again.

Aunty Iris suddenly got up. She went to the sideboard, opened a cupboard and took out the fruit bowl.

Alistair and Uncle Bob stared. Colin was surprised too.

Aunty Iris only got the fruit bowl out on very special occasions.

She held it out to Ted.

'Here, love,' she said, 'have one of these. Take your mind off things.'

Colin saw that inside the bowl were five tangerines.

Ted took one, and slowly his face began to crumple. Great sobs shook his body.

Aunty Iris and Uncle Bob and Alistair stared in

horror. Then Aunty Iris nudged Uncle Bob and Uncle Bob hurried Alistair out of the room.

'Would you like another cup of tea now?' asked Aunty Iris.

Ted opened his mouth to try and answer but he couldn't, so massive and heartfelt were his sobs.

Colin tried to answer for him.

No good.

Colin felt his own body shudder and his own face crumple and his own tears spill out of his eyes.

Not anger this time, but grief.

And as he wept, grief and sadness running out of him in bucketfuls, and as he watched Ted doing the same, it wasn't Mum and Dad he was thinking of, or himself.

It was Luke.

Chapter Sixteen

Next morning at breakfast Colin told them.

Aunty Iris froze in the middle of requesting Alistair not to pick his pimples at the table.

Uncle Bob froze just as he was about to ask Alistair if he'd heard what his mother had just said.

Colin told them again.

'I want to go home and be with Luke.'

Aunty Iris and Uncle Bob looked at each other.

'You can't, love,' said Aunty Iris gently.

'You don't really want to go back to all that, do you?' said Uncle Bob.

'Yes,' said Colin.

'He does,' said Alistair.

'Alistair eat your breakfast,' said Aunty Iris. 'Love, your Mum and Dad want you to be here. They think it's best for you.'

'I've got to go, Aunty Iris.'

'See.'

'Shut up, Alistair.'

'Please, Uncle Bob.'

'Let him.'

'You heard what your mother said, Alistair.'

Alistair slammed his fist onto the table. Cups, saucers and both his parents jumped into the air.

'He's going,' said Alistair, looking steadily at his mother and father, 'and that's final.'

Colin stared at Alistair, amazed.

Uncle Bob and Aunty Iris stared at Alistair, dumbfounded.

Alistair, breathless, grinned proudly at Colin.

There was a long silence in which Aunty Iris and Uncle Bob opened their mouths several times to speak to Alistair and then closed them again.

'Listen to me, Colin,' said Aunty Iris finally. 'You're not going to Australia and that's that. And just in case you've got any notions of going to the airport, don't waste your time. They won't let you on the plane without us to sign the forms.'

The morning after that, just before breakfast, Colin went to the airport.

He woke early, packed, said goodbye to Alistair, wrote down directions when Alistair said he was coming to Australia as soon as he'd figured how to get the new lock off the back door, left Alistair the screwdriver, crept downstairs while Aunty Iris and Uncle Bob were in the bathroom, left a note in the hall ('Gone for a walk. Cricket training. Be a while.') and slipped out the front door which Uncle Bob had unlocked to get the paper.

At the end of the street he felt a hand on his shoulder.

He froze.

Then he turned round.

It was the postman, smiling cheerily.

'You Colin Mudford from number 86?' he asked.

Colin nodded, heart pounding.

The postman handed him a letter.

'Friends in high places, eh?' said the postman, walking off.

The letter was from Buckingham Palace.

Colin stuffed it into his pocket. He'd read it later. He had a plane to catch.

Ted was waiting for him at Heathrow airport.

'Just as well you rang when you did,' said Ted, 'I'm off to Wales for the funeral later today.'

Colin was about to put his bag on the conveyor belt at the check-in counter.

He stopped.

'I should really come with you,' he said.

Ted put the bag onto the conveyor belt.

'You should go where you're going,' he said.

The man at the counter checked Colin's ticket and Ted signed the forms to allow Colin to get on the plane without an adult accompanying him.

'What relationship are you to the traveller?' the man at the counter asked Ted.

'Mate,' said Colin.

'Friend,' said Ted.

'Guardian?' asked the man.

'That's right,' said Colin.

Just before they parted at customs, Colin gave Ted

his present. A scarf. He'd bought it from a stall at the underground station. It was pink.

'My favourite colour,' said Ted, putting it on.

Colin grinned. He'd always liked pink but blokes didn't wear it where he came from.

He decided not to make a meal of saying goodbye. Just a hug and a grin, and Ted flipped the scarf over his shoulder and was gone.

'Bloody queen,' said a man behind Colin.

Colin turned and looked the man right in the eyes. 'He's not,' he said, 'but he should be.'

Over Yugoslavia Colin opened the letter from the person who was.

Dear Mr Mudford, it said, *Her Majesty's sympathies are with all who suffer through illness. May I, on her behalf, wish your brother a speedy recovery.*

It was signed by a Palace Liaison Officer.

Colin left it in the ashtray.

Colin stopped outside Luke's room and took a deep breath.

He looked in through the glass panel in the door.

There was Luke, in bed, surrounded by hospital equipment. He looked smaller than Colin remembered, and very pale. His hair was sort of wispy.

There were Mum and Dad sitting on either side of the bed talking to Luke. They looked pale as well. And tired.

Colin took another deep breath and walked in.

He didn't even look at Mum and Dad, and barely heard their amazed gasps.

Plenty of time for that later.

He just looked at Luke, who was staring at him in delight, sitting up in bed, flinging his arms round his neck, squealing his name joyously, hugging him as if he'd never let go.

Colin felt the tears pouring down his cheeks and he didn't even try to stop them.

There wasn't a person in the world he would have changed places with at that moment, not even the Queen of England.